The Dream Drifters

Diane Banham

The Dream Drifters

Cover design by Leanne Brown at Sirenic Creations

Imagination can take you anywhere

Copyright © 2019 Diane Banham

All rights reserved.

No part of this book may be reproduced in any form
including information storage and retrieval systems
without permission in writing from the publisher.

dianebanhamimagine@outlook.com

For Tim, Thomas and William.

Without your patience and support this book may

never exist.

Love you more …

Chapter 1

Jack

"JACK RUN!" came the cry from the three tiny faces watching the moonlit chase as they flew high above the trees. Jack didn't hear them, he didn't even know they were there. "HURRY! WE'RE JUST IN TIME" as the little red dragon carrying them on her back dropped like a stone through the swaying evil tree branches. Dodging and darting between the grabbing stick fingers she flew down to where an exhausted Jack lay.

With his face covered in dirt, Jack lay still for a moment as warm salty tears ran down his face. His heart thumped louder than ever, and his shin stung from where he had banged it on a fallen branch.

The ground shook more and more as the crashing noise right behind him got louder and louder, when suddenly it stopped. Jack could feel the monster's warm and very smelly breath on the back of his neck.

Turning over slowly Jack gulped as standing before him were a pair of giant hairy feet. He followed them up with his tear-filled eyes until he reached the face of the monster that was towering over him its hot breath raining down on him. A small boy sat all alone in his dirty pyjamas, on the forest floor.

The monster stared at him for a moment as its drool dripped onto the floor with a loud splat from its giant mouth. Leaning forward it lowered its head, sniffing Jack as if deciding if he smelt good enough to eat.

PPPPPPAAAARRRRPPPPPPPP!!

The monster trumped so loudly the ground rumbled like an earthquake, as a thick green fog appeared. Jack's eyes began to sting, and the smell was so bad he began to feel faint. It sneered through its big yellow moldy teeth. This little boy would make a very tasty treat indeed as it opened its mouth wide ready to gobble Jack up.

"NO" screamed Jack throwing his muddy hands up in front of his face and closing his sore eyes.

"NOW" came the cry. The tiny red dragon and its passengers flew like a dazzling bolt of lightning directly between Jack and the huge monster's mouth, startling the beast and causing it to stop and take a step back.

Like a firework with a red hot glowing tail, they flew around and around the monster's head, darting in front of its face, shooting out hot sparks and fire, making it back further away in surprise and more importantly, further away from Jack.

Peeping through his shaking dirty fingers at the commotion Jack was just in time to see the dragon fly directly towards the monster's eyes.

"GET READY" came the yell as one of the tiny people onboard threw something into the air. There was an almighty bang followed by a blinding bright light that made the monster roar in surprise. It stumbled backwards rubbing its dazzled eyes hard.

Jack watched in disbelief as the dragon flew down, landing on the branch he had stumbled over, and the three tiny people onboard slid off it's back.

"Hi Jack" one said waving, "it's really nice to see you again. Sorry we were a little late it's so windy up there tonight" she said pointing up through the trees. She ignored the huge monster now stumbling around behind them crashing into trees and moaning. "*Pooeeyyy* and if I may say it's a little windy down here as well," she said pinching her nose from the smelly fog that was still lingering in the air.

"Oh no need to worry about him he can't see thanks to Noggins' Flashcrash Grenade," said another pointing towards the monster and smiling. "It's a bit like when you look at a glowing light bulb and then all you can see is a bright light for a while afterwards. First, there is a flash and then you crash. It will however wear off, so we will have to be quick."

With a mix of complete shock and confusion on his face, Jack got to his hands and knees and leant down closer to the tiny people so he could see them clearly.

"Who *are* you and what do you mean see you *again*?" he questioned as the monster fell over a tree backwards, knocking it to the ground with an almighty crash.

"Oh, I'm sorry how rude of us, sometimes I forget you don't remember," said one of the figures walking forward a little. "Let me make the introductions, my names Fitz," he said placing a hand on his chest. "This is Noggin and that is Snitch" as he pointed to the other two in turn who waved and smiled back at Jack. "And this is Ember," he said patting the tiny red dragon on the neck who gave a puff of smoke and a nod. "We're here to help" he announced proudly.

"O-o-o of course you are" stuttered Jack not quite believing what he was seeing. He was still a little confused as he could not remember ever meeting the tiny people stood before him, and surely, he would remember something as crazy as that he thought.

Beyond them, the monster was now getting clumsily back to his feet. As it rubbed its stinging eyes, it could just make out the boy on the ground a short distance before him. It could not however, see the tiny rescuers on the branch. The monster as you can imagine was now very, very cross and even more determined to gobble up Jack.

"Oh boy HERE HE COMES!" cried Snitch looking towards the monster as it stumbled towards them with anger in its eyes. The smell of its rotten cabbage breath was lingering in the air and the green stinky fog clung to the air behind its hairy bottom.

"Well, Jack it was lovely meeting you," said Fitz hurriedly "but now you have to trust us" as he removed the backpack he was wearing and turned to face the monster.

Jack watched curiously as Fitz carefully took from his bag a small, milky white glowing pearl and held it out before him in both hands. The monster was now rambling towards them all at high speed, it's dribbling mouth open and growling loudly.

"Watch this Jack, you're going to love it," said Noggin with excitement. As the monster reached the fallen branch and grabbed at the again terrified Jack, Fitz ripped open the pearl holding half in each hand with his arms wide apart.

In an instant, there was a giant blast of icy wind shooting up into the air with an almighty rushing sound like an explosion. It was such a blast it blew Fitz's hair up on end as the wind shot up his face causing him to shut his eyes tight. This was followed by an extremely loud sucking and gurgling noise that Jack thought sounded just like the water swirling down the bath plug hole at home.

The monster froze motionless in mid-air and looked down at Jack with surprise, followed by a look of horror that spread across its face. Rolling its eyes downwards it finally saw the three tiny people below its huge hairy feet who were now waving and grinning from ear to ear.

"Bye, Bye" waved Snitch and Noggin both laughing as the monster and everything around it started to swirl and swirl being pulled into the tiny pearl that Fitz held tightly in his hands. The woods, the scary trees, the moon, even the dark sky, everything was being pulled in like a giant swirling tornado.

Jack sat down and pulled his knees tight up to his chest, closed his eyes tightly and threw his hands over his ears as the swirling cold air rushed around him.

Silence…

Turning over on his pillow Jack snuggled back down to sleep, warm and cosy with his alarm clock ticking softly at his bedside. The moonlight outside crept in through a gap in the curtains which blew gently in the cool night breeze from an open window. On the bed sat Noggin and Snitch with Ember waiting patiently by the clock as they had many times before and, no doubt, would do many times again.

"Well, that's another successful night" whispered Fitz as he opened his backpack very carefully so as not to damage the cargo inside. Nestling in the bag were two pearls, one that had been white and glowing in the forest but was now black as night and swirling with the nightmare monster trapped within. Beside it lay another even smaller pearl that was golden and shimmered with a million rainbow colours reflecting in the moonlight as he lifted it out.

"I love this bit" whispered Snitch as Fitz crept quietly past the sleeping Jack so as not to disturb him. Disappearing for a moment under the corner of the pillow he returned without the tiny pearl, which he left slightly cracked open, safely underneath.

"There, one Dream Pearl delivered safe and sound. I hope it's a fun dream Jack" said Fitz in relief.

"Sweet dreams" whispered Noggin as Ember flew out of the open window carrying the three homeward bound into the starry night sky, leaving Jack smiling in his sleep.

Jack stretched hard under his covers as he woke, the morning sunshine beamed through his curtains and felt warm on his sleepy face. He'd had the best night's sleep and the most amazing dream about running down a white sandy beach barefoot with his pet dog Finn. They were playing in a crystal clear warm blue ocean in the sunshine, Jack could still feel the warm water between his toes.

He did not remember the big smelly monster trying to eat him or the scary forest or running scared… He did not remember the three tiny people on their faithful red dragon, but then again…. he never did.

Chapter 2

Dolomite Dell

Louder and louder and louder....

DING A LING A LING A LING A

LING!!!

Fitz opened one blurry eye slowly under the warm soft covers with his face scrunched deep into his pillow, he had been having a simply amazing dream. What was that awful noise that was disturbing him so rudely?

Without having a moment to think about the answer the bed covers suddenly shot completely off the end of the bed. A shocked Fitz instantly sat bolt upright as the cold air hit his skin covering him goose bumps, both his sleepy eyes were now wide open as he realised exactly what the noise was.

"OH NO NOT AGAIN!" he yelled as his alarm clock whizzed past his head.

Its big brass rimmed white face was shining in the sunbeams coming through the window and its two black clock hands were spinning around at high speed. A pair of tiny white feathered wings were flapping so fast they were like a blur and two big brass bells on the top rang loudly as it shot past Fitz with a very mischievous grin on its cheeky face.

First, the clock hit the floor and then shot up to the ceiling, before bouncing off all the walls knocking everything over that got in its way.

DING A LING A LING A LING A

LING!!!

Leaping off the bed Fitz frantically chased the naughty clock around the room desperately trying to catch it. Banging his big toe hard on the bed the burning pain made him grab his foot, causing him to get caught up in the bedcovers that were now in a pile on the floor and knocking even more things over in the process. The room looked like a messy bomb had exploded.

"NO STOP!" he shouted at the top of his voice desperately as the tiny clock flew past his ear and straight out of the open bedroom window.

Shaking his head Fitz watched as the clock stopped mid-air, turned towards him, stuck out its tongue, blew a *very* loud raspberry, did a cheeky little bow then turned and flew away merrily into the bright blue sky still ringing loudly as it went.

DING A LING A LING A LING A LING!!!

"And there goes another one," he sighed rubbing his sore toe as the ringing clock disappeared into the distance. "I wonder where they all go?" he pondered.

Rubbing the dried sleep from his tired eyes he ran his fingers through his mop of black hair and looked out of the bedroom window across his home Dolomite Dell.

Dolomite Dell is a wondrous magical place on a floating island way, way up in the sky. The island floats on a sea of white clouds and the Dolomite crystals that give it its name shimmer and sparkle like millions of diamonds.

As their day is our night here on Earth you may mistake it for a star in the night sky but which one it is, well that's a secret.

Row upon row of tiny houses in every colour of the rainbow with brick red tiled roofs, white windows and flowers growing round the little doors are squashed up, almost on top of one another, through steep narrow cobbled winding streets that are lit by tiny fireflies at night. They reach high up the hillside from the warm white sandy beach at

Cloud Bay before they change colour to the greens and browns of the forest.

Here they twist and turn their way down through the leafy glades and cool tracks of the lush green forest dell with its babbling streams, tiny blue darting dragonflies and canopy of giant green leaves and ferns. They stretch all the way to the bottom of Dreamcast Mountain, which rises majestically grey and rugged at the centre of the island.

This is the home of the Dream Drifters, tiny people who are sent to Earth as we sleep by The Guardians.

They are the protectors of our dreams and captors of our nightmares, which they keep under lock and key deep in the Granite Vault safe from harm, or so we thought.

Chapter 3

Ember

It was another busy morning with Dream Drifters everywhere all going about their days work, rushing here and there. Today something seemed different thought a sleepy Fitz as he looked around, there were groups of people whispering together in little huddles and looking very worried indeed.

"HEY SLEEPY HEAD! LET'S GO" came a shout from far below the window. There stood Fitz's best friends and the other two members of his team; Noggin with her untamed red hair, sparkling green eyes, freckles and rosy cheeks and Snitch with his wild fluffy white hair that always looked like he'd had an electric shock and black framed glasses that magnified his eyes making them look twice as big as they should be. Both of them had their hands across their mouths trying desperately not to laugh.

"IT'S NOT FUNNY" shouted back Fitz smiling. "That's the 3rd alarm clock this week I've lost."

Leaving the sound of Noggin and Snitch laughing loudly below Fitz quickly got dressed. Grabbing his backpack that was still dirty from their last adventure with Jack, he rushed out of the door and into the bright morning sunshine.

"Come on! Hurry up slowcoach!" called back Noggin over her shoulder as she took off running fast along the street, her red and white long striped legs flashing in the sunlight and black boots clicking on the cobbles. Following was Snitch puffing hard as however hard he tried he struggled to keep up as his legs were a little bit shorter.

They headed down through the winding house lined streets, leaping across the bubbling streams on moss covered stepping stones, ducking under giant leaves that hung over the pathways and dodging the giant drops of morning dew sent rolling down them by tiny sparkles of darting light called Dew Dancers.

Dew Dancers are in fact cheeky sprites with wings who are even smaller than the Dream Drifters. They come to earth as we sleep in the breaking light of the early morning and dance around sprinkling their dew on the ground and plants, decorating the spiderwebs with water crystals making them sparkle like magic. They are *very* naughty, and their favourite game is to wet the Dream Drifters as they run by them in the Dell.

Slamming his front door shut behind him Fitz set off after them as fast as he could. "Hey, wait for me! What's happening and why is everyone looking so worried?" he called, struggling to put his backpack on whilst trying to keep up.

"We don't know exactly but the word is something really bad has happened at Dreamcast Mountain" puffed Snitch over his shoulder with a bead of sweat running down his red face. A giant drop of dew rolled off a leaf and landed on his head with a splosh and then ran down his neck in a cooling trickle. "For once that actually feels quite nice" he sighed followed by a giggle from the naughty sprites.

Finally, Fitz caught up just as the three of them arrived on the white sand of Cloud Bay, where Snitch screeched to a halt causing Fitz to almost fall over him.

"Oh boy, I really hate this part" he groaned rubbing his wet hair as his face turned pale.

There in front of them appearing up through the billowing white cloud sea was the team of

Guardian's Dream Dragons. Each one landing silently with a rush of wind on the beach before them. On each dragon's back lay a beautiful golden leather saddle shining in the sunlight with three seats ready to transport the Dream Drifter teams to wherever they were needed.

Fearless Noggin was already climbing aboard their dragon. She was an elegant tall fire red dragon called Ember whose deep green eyes sparkled like the purest emeralds. Almost like real flames, her scales shimmered from the darkest red through to the brightest orange as she stood proudly on the white sand.

"Come on! Hurry up scaredy pants" called Noggin from her front seat, looking down at Snitch with a naughty twinkle in her eye as Fitz climbed aboard.

Snitch gulped, took a deep breath to steady himself and clambered aboard Ember. Quickly he climbed into the back seat behind Fitz, closed his eyes and hung on so tightly his fingers went white. After checking all three were safely aboard Ember crouched down on her mighty legs and with a swoop of her enormous wings took off.

"I HATE FLYING!" squealed Snitch as he turned green and squeezed his fingers even tighter.

"WAHOOO!" shouted Noggin as she fearlessly waved one arm in the air above her head "What do you mean this is the best part?"

Ember soared through the air at speed around the bay dodging all the other flying dragons that were carrying teams to the mountain top. Swooping low across the Dell, they skimmed the giant leaves, making the Dream Drifters in the streets below duck as her gust of wind blew off their tiny hats and ruffled their hair. With a puff of smoke, she scared the cheeky Dew Dancers before flying straight up and to the top of Dreamcast Mountain.

Folding her wings, she dropped down inside a large opening in the mountaintop, landing gracefully on one of the many platforms that stuck out from the mountain inside.

Fitz and Noggin immediately slid out of their seats and off Ember's back hurriedly walking towards a large round door in the mountain side. Behind them, Ember gave a snort and they turned to find Snitch still hanging onto his seat, eyes closed tightly as he shook like a jelly.

"You can open your eyes now," called Fitz whilst Noggin tried and failed to hide a giggle beside him. Snitch did not move.

"You know on Earth they have things called airplanes for this where you get to sit in a nice comfortable seat, warm inside and not on a scaly bumpy thing like a dragon" he snapped. "They even serve you drinks!"

With this Ember turned and promptly sat down which caused Snitch to lose his grip on his seat. As

29

he bounced down her rough scaly back, he screwed up his face in pain before hitting the ground hard with a loud bump.

"Well, that's just great," snapped Snitch crossly "What a way to start a day, a bruised bottom." Noggin and Fitz burst out laughing whilst Ember simply snorted in disgust and flew away leaving a sore Snitch sat on the floor.

Above, below and all around them, the other Dream Dragons were landing, each with their own team of Dream Drifters aboard.

"Looks like everyone has been summoned, that can't be good," said Snitch as he got to his feet and looked at Fitz who was nodding slowly, a deep look of worry across his face.

Chapter 4

Guardians

Approaching the mighty round door Fitz took off his backpack and reaching inside the front pocket. He took out a small blue pearl, which swirled in the light like it held an entire ocean inside. Carefully he dropped the pearl into a small hole just to the side of the door where it rolled inside for a second then disappeared completely.

After a moment there was a loud clank and groan as a maze of secret hidden locks within the door itself started to undo and then slowly, it swung open on giant hinges with a loud creak.

Inside lay a small room carved from the mountain stone and in the centre hung a lamp that glowed warmly from the firefly flittering inside, making the dolomite crystals in the rock sparkle like glitter.

Directly on the wall opposite were two golden lockers one said '**FITZ**' and the other '**NOGGIN**' in bold black letters. A stone table stood next to them and on the top stood a beautiful carved wooden chest with golden hinges and a clasp with the name '**SNITCH**' on the lid.

Two pairs of night vision goggles hung on the walls and, to the right, was a dark circular opening to the tunnel slide with a small pile of mats next to it. This slide leads down to the Guardians and the Granite Vault buried deep below them inside the depths of the island itself. From the opening, they heard the sound of faint panicked echoing voices, doors slamming and people's footsteps rushing around way below.

"That doesn't sound good," said a concerned Fitz to the others.

Noggin and Fitz each ran to their lockers. Fitz was the team leader and, on opening his locker lifted out a purple velvet bag tied with a golden silk thread. Inside lay an empty Dream Catcher Pearl like the one he had used for Jack's scary nightmare, carefully he placed it in his backpack.

Fearless Noggin was in charge of the team's tools and gadgets. She strapped on a utility belt weighed down full of magical gadgets and gizmos the team would need for any adventure.

Snitch was the team's knowledge keeper and knew everything about everything (well almost). He had access to the Guardian's vast Library of Knowledge, created over many centuries containing everything they had learnt about the big wide world floating below them.

Opening the wooden box, he lifted out a pair of black gloves which he slipped on, then clapped his hands together and wiggled his fingers. The gloves and Snitch's glasses frames burst into life as if they were linked together. Both shimmered with tiny crackles of silver and purple light, almost like tiny electricity bolts shooting through them. Then as fast as the lights had appeared, they disappeared, and the gloves and glasses were back to black.

Slamming their locker doors shut and closing the box lid carefully Noggin and Fitz grabbed a pair of the night vision goggles then one by one they took a small mat from the pile on the floor and launched themselves into the dark hole of the tunnel slide.

Twisting and turning they shot down the polished slippery slide at speed, shooting around and around the tube towards the small dot of light at the bottom, which got bigger and bigger until they finally shot out landing with a thud in the corridor below.

Waiting impatiently for their arrival stood three of the Guardians who lived inside the mountain, each dressed head to toe in white robes with just their hairy toes sticking out underneath. The Guardians were usually very calm and quiet people who spoke softly, but not today.

"You have to come with us immediately," said one with white spiky hair a bit like a hedgehog. On the end of his round, rosy nose and balancing on his freckled red plump cheeks were perched a pair of large gold rimmed glasses. From his chin dangled a white beard shaped exactly like a question mark.

"No time to lose, hurry, hurry!" said another who was taller and thinner with long white hair twisted around his head almost like a tall pointed hat. From his chin hung a long thin pointy beard that went right down to his belly button, if Guardians do have belly buttons that is.

"We thought you would never get here, hurry he's waiting" cried the third impatiently waving his hands. With lots of white hair and a beard that looked like someone had a big bubble bath then dropped all the bubbles on his head and around his chin Snitch was not sure where the bubble hair stopped, and the bubbly beard started.

"Who's waiting, what's happened?" asked Fitz loudly trying to be heard over all the commotion going on around them.

"They came, they came in the night. How could this happen, how did we not see them coming? *It's a disaster*" wailed the three Guardians as they hurried Fitz, Noggin and Snitch to their feet and along the corridor towards the huge Granite Vault.

Chapter 5

The Granite Vault

More and more Dream Drifter teams were arriving popping out of their slides all along the corridor. In the chaos, they were almost falling over each other as all the Guardians rushed around in a panic. There were people everywhere dashing in and out of the doors stretching along the walls as far as you could see.

Snitch was right, something bad had happened, very bad. Then, in all the confusion out of the corner of his eye, Fitz saw him, very briefly and almost like a ghost but he definitely saw him, stood tall in the glowing light of one of the wall lamps much further along the corridor. Noggin saw him as well and took in a sharp breath.

"Night Warrior…" she whispered slowly under her breath, he turned as if he heard her looking directly at them, but in a blink, he vanished.

With this, the three Guardians were again hurrying the team along the corridor and around the corner towards the entrance of the Granite vault. This was usually locked shut with a round thick cast iron door, a pair of dragon wings engraved on it, but when they turned the corner instead of it standing proudly protecting the entrance to the vault it was lying on the floor all bent and twisted. The door looked like it had been ripped from its hinges by a giant's hand.

"SEE, SEE!" cried the three Guardians pointing at the twisted mangled door. *"Oh, how could he, how could this happen?"* they wailed again with their heads in their hands.

Fitz, Snitch and Noggin looked at each other all very confused and with a tight feeling of panic inside they rushed through the broken door and into the Granite Vault beyond.

Inside the circular vault, the walls spiral up and up as far as the eye can see, with row upon row of Dream Pearls all golden and shimmering with rainbow colours almost as if they were alive, each one holding a happy dream.

These golden pearls are used by the Dream Drifter teams on their nightly missions to Earth, where they are sent by the Guardians to capture peoples' nightmares. These are removed forever and replaced instead with a wonderful dream hidden inside a golden Dream Pearl.

The dream inside is created just for that person by the Guardians and no one else, they are left under your pillow whilst you sleep, cracked open to release the dream within. Of course, they are so tiny we never feel them and after we wake, the pearls completely disappear so we never even know they existed. The shimmering golden rainbow coloured light of these pearls reflects on the walls and floor of the vault, making it sparkle and dance like the truly magical place it is.

Fitz, Noggin and Snitch burst into the room and stopped expecting there to be a disaster awaiting them but to their surprise, everything was the same as it should be.

There in the centre of the glistening room stood the leader of the Guardians, the High Minister. Slightly bent over wearing long swaying white robes with his long silky floor length white hair, moustache, bushy white eyebrows and beard leaving nothing showing but his kind old eyes. In his hands he gripped a long white walking stick topped by a clear crystal that was crafted from a single dragon's tear. He stood very still in silence, hands together propped on his stick, waiting patiently.

"High Minister what's happened?" asked Fitz walking further into the vault and looking around still very confused. At the far side of the vault lay an eerie area of shadowy darkness he had not seen before.

"Why is the vault open, the door crushed and *who* came in the night?" whispered Snitch as he looked around feeling scared and not really wanting to know the answer to his question.

"Solomon Fear" replied a deep voice from the darkness and as the High Minister turned, footsteps echoed around the vault and brought the person hiding in the shadows into the light.

Walking towards them was a person they have never seen but had heard tales of since they were young, never knowing if they were true or just made up fairy stories. The leader of the Night Warriors Bysidian Black stood before them.

Chapter 6

Bysidian Black

He was a tall thin man with long silver hair tied back in a sleek ponytail his face scarred from battles.

Dressed head to toe in jet black shining armour and draped around his shoulders hung a silver and black cape, on his hands were battered black leather gloves and, on his feet, long scuffed black boots. By his side hung an elegant sword carved from a dragon's fang, the blade engraved with flames and in the handle lay a purple crystal that shone in the Dream Pearls light. He stopped next to the High Minister.

"Are you sure they are the right ones for the job?" he questioned with a disbelieving frown on his face. The High Minister nodded once in reply but did not speak.

"Excuse me but did you say Solomon Fear?" gulped a scared Snitch whispering the name as he dare not say it out loud. Bysidian Black looked down at him with piercing blue eyes, whilst Noggin poked him in the ribs unable to speak herself. She was bursting with excitement inside and was afraid she might explode if she made a sound.

"Follow me" demanded Bysidian after a moment, walking off into the eerie darkness he had appeared from with a swish of his cloak. The trio started to follow but stopped short of the shadows having lost sight of him.

"Wow, he's so fast, where did he go?" asked Fitz.

"Well, I am not going in there" proclaimed Snitch stubbornly "no way, no way." As he shook his head he started to turn and move back towards the light, when in a flash a black armoured hand appeared from the dark and grabbed him by the arm, pulling a squealing Snitch into the darkness beyond.

"SNITCH" they cried in panic as Fitz and Noggin ran bravely into the darkness. They ran and ran much further than they thought possible surely, they would find the Granite Vault wall soon. As they turned back, they could just make out the faint glow of the Dream Pearls in the distance, but their light was not bright enough to reach where they stood.

Loud blubbering noises came from somewhere ahead and following the sound they eventually came across Bysidian Black and Snitch. The low glow of a lamp resting on the floor shone upwards and lit their faces in the otherwise pitch-black space.

"Where did this darkness come from and *what* is that?" questioned Fitz trying not to show his fear. Just in front of them almost visible in the light but not clearly, they could just make out a shape, large and round with a chilling cold wind blowing from it just like the Dream Catcher Pearls when Fitz opened them.

"That," said Bysidian pointing "is the vault you did not know exists, the vault beyond the Granite Vault that we Night Warriors are here to protect and serve.

It is that creating this darkness you see leaking into the Granite Vault."

Slowly raising the lamp from the floor, he revealed another huge round iron door, or what was left of it at least with a large screaming face of terror carved into the front. As with the Granite Vault the door was almost destroyed, hanging on one hinge almost bent in half and open enough for someone to just get inside.

"W-w-what is in there?" asked Noggin stammering, she was always so brave and strong, but she had an awful feeling inside that frightened her, and she didn't want to show it.

In the dim lamplight Fitz looked at his team, they were all scared, but they had been picked by the High Minister for some reason he thought, and he wanted to know more.

"Stay with me at all times" instructed Bysidian in a low quiet voice and carrying the lamp, he climbed slowly through the gap in the broken door into the dark cold space beyond.

Chapter 7

Swirling Fog

Inside the air was so cold you could see your breath and wind whistled around the walls making the whole place appear to moan and wail.

Unexpectedly in the darkness, there suddenly appeared a blinding light where Bysidian stood as he produced a small purple crystal from his armour. Placing it in the palm of his outstretched hand the crystal started to rise into the air. Higher and higher until they almost lost sight of it. After a moment a dark purple glow appeared from somewhere way up high and fell like purple rain until the whole room was bathed in its dim light.

The inside of the vault looked very similar to the Guardians Granite Vault. Circular in shape but smaller and it narrowed as the walls reached upwards. The ceiling was so high it disappeared into the darkness, if indeed there was a ceiling there at all. Here though instead of all the pearls shimmering and being golden they were black as night, with a thick swirling fog around each one making the air feel damp.

Below their feet carved into the cold hard stone floor was a huge dragon's face. It stared back at them its mouth wide open, fangs sharp with staring eyes. The eyes were carved into the stone but in the centre where the slit like pupils should be there was instead deep black holes, with the wind whistling out of them.

The trio stood shivering, open-mouthed and wide-eyed when in the silence Noggin started to sniff. The sniffing got louder and louder as it echoed around the room followed by warm fat salty tears that starting to run down her cheeks. Noggin quickly wiped them away hoping none of the others had seen but another appeared, then another and another, until they ran like a small river down her face and dripped off her chin. Then the sobbing started, louder and louder until she was crying so hard her chest and throat hurt. Fitz looked at her in disbelief, she had never ever cried before, well not that he had seen anyway.

Without warning, a hot rush of anger shot into Fitz's toes making them tingle. The burning feeling rushed up through his legs and body right to his head and shot out of his mouth with a blast.

"WHAT ARE YOU DOING YOU WIMP?" he screamed at Noggin, blood boiling in his very red face with angry eyes staring out from underneath his frowning eyebrows.

From his other side Snitch suddenly started to scream uncontrollably. With his hands grasping his cheeks he was holding his face hard with a look of absolute terror in his eyes as if he was in his worst nightmare.

Snatching his cape from around his neck Bysidian quickly swirled it through the air and threw it over all three of them, covering them from head to toe like a large blanket.

"Give it a moment, don't panic you will be fine in a second just wait". The cape began to turn from thick black cloth to completely clear, they could see out of it as clear as glass as if it were not even there, but they knew it was as they could feel its weight draped over them. Gradually the sniffing subsided, the tears dried, the anger fell away and the fear started to disappear.

"Sorry," said Bysidian "I forgot you would need protection from the power of the pearls. My armour does that for me, and it's been so long since anyone other than a night warrior came into here. Don't worry my cape will shield you for a short time."

"What is this place and what's happening to us?" asked Fitz deeply concerned for his team who were all a little shocked by what had just happened.

Bysidian took a deep breath, his eyes slowly moved around the room and rested on the destroyed door.

"At night," he started to explain in a low voice. "When you return from your missions to the other world with your Dream Catcher Pearls all black and full of the nightmares that you have trapped, what do you think happens to them?"

"Well, we hand them to the Guardians and from then I have never really thought to ask, I don't know where they go" replied Fitz shaking his head.

"Well, we sure do now," said Noggin looking around.

"Your job is to capture the nightmares in your empty pearls, replacing them with a full golden Dream Pearl from the Guardians. You make sure people have happy dreams, well as Night Warriors our duty is to banish the nightmares you return with" continued Bysidian.

At this point, Snitch decided he did not really want to know anymore as it was all getting far too scary. Slowly he stretched his right leg out backwards hoping to turn and run, but once his leg was outside the cloak covering them the urge to scream returned again. Slowly he pulled his leg back under cover hoping Bysidian and the others had not noticed.

"Banish" questioned Noggin who was not sure she liked that word. "What do you mean?"

"We are here to fight the contents of those black pearls," Bysidian said pointing at the rows and rows before them. With this, the pearls seemed to glow blacker as if they knew they were being spoken about. Fitz gulped, Noggins mouth dropped, and Snitch simply sat down hard in shock as his legs wobbled like jelly.

"You actually fight what's inside," said Fitz slowly and in disbelief.

"My team of warriors and I do, yes" replied Bysidian. "Once they are trapped the nightmares within get stronger and stronger as they gain power, we have to destroy them for good as the pearls can only hold them prisoner for so long before they risk cracking or even worse exploding. If they split and release the new more powerful nightmare back onto the world who knows what will happen."

Snitch shuddered, he certainly did not want to meet some more powerful versions of the nightmares they had trapped over time, the originals had been scary enough for him thank you.

"Wow" whispered Noggin slowly a twinkle in her eye and this time it was not a tear. She was always the fearless crazy one on the team, not afraid of anything and never listened to anyone, not even Fitz all the time.

Snitch got to his feet from the cold hard floor shaking his head slowly. "And here it comes" he sighed knowing exactly what was about to spill from Noggins mouth.

"You know," started Noggin looking at Bysidian and the others "I knew I was destined for greater things, a Night Warrior sounds just *BRILLIANT!*" she shouted screwing up her face and punching the air almost knocking the cloak off. Turning she looked at Fitz, but he was not listening, Fitz was looking straight past her at something else.

"Helloooooo," said Noggin waving a hand in front of his face a little annoyed at being ignored. She turned to Snitch who, open mouthed and very pale, was also now staring in the same direction. Noggin turned and following both their gazes she stopped in her tracks.

There was a gap in the string of nightmares.

A pearl was missing.

Chapter 8

Adventure Beckons

All around them the room began to darken, slowly at first then darker and darker until they could hardly see.

"Hurry," said Bysidian "my cloaks powers are fading we need to leave right now."

With a mighty sigh of relief, they turned and abandoned the cloak for Bysidian to pick up. As they ran through the twisted door, they turned to see that it had already returned to black as Bysidian followed them through the shadows and back to the safety of the Granite Vault. The High Minister was still waiting.

"WAIT" demanded an angry Fitz raising his hand as he puffed hard trying to catch his breath from running out of that awful place. "You need to tell us *right now* what is happening, why are we here and if someone doesn't tell us the truth we are leaving?"

Shuffling forward the High Minister spoke "We need your help. Last night Solomon Fear and his band of Pirates attacked Dreamcast Mountain, they got through our defences into the Nightmare Vault and stole a Nightmare Pearl."

Bysidian continued. "The pearl he stole has my team of Night Warriors inside battling a nightmare, but they need my help to do that. Now they are trapped inside until it is returned to the vault for me to release them. If Solomon has the pearl and manages to open it then the nightmare within will be released back into the open. It will be much stronger and even more fearsome than before. My team will stand no chance of defeating it or escaping with their lives."

Snitch frowned with suspicion "Hold on a second if your team needed your help, why were you not in the pearl with them?".

"As I was about to follow my men inside Solomon and his band of pirates struck. It was as if they knew our defences were weak and had been waiting until my men were gone." Bysidian bowed his head in shame. "I stayed to try and defend the Guardians and the vault, but the pirates were too strong for me alone."

"I knew it" exclaimed Noggin. "You need me to become a Night Warrior and help you" she cried as a glint of adventure and excitement shone in her eye.

Snitch rolled his eyes and shook his head in utter disbelief as there was a moment of silence.

"You want us to get the pearl, back don't you?" asked Fitz calmly realising why they were there.

"Yes, yes we do" nodded the High Minister. "We need your help as you're the best team we have. We cannot send Bysidian, we need him here in case Solomon and his men return."

At first, Snitch could hear voices that seemed quiet and muffled, then they got louder and louder and clearer and clearer. Why was everything black and why did his head hurt? He smiled as he realised, he must be dreaming, yes that was it, of course, none of this was real and right now he was all snuggled up and fast asleep in his big cosy bed. He must be having a nightmare of his own, even though Dream Drifters do not actually have nightmares at all, or do they but never remember?

"Come on Snitch wake up, WAKE UP" as he felt his body shaking from side to side. Suddenly eyes wide open he woke. Fitz was staring at him closely in the face shaking him hard. Behind him jumping around like someone had lit a firework in her pants was Noggin.

"*YAHOOO, YAHOO!*" she shouted over and over "I knew it, I knew it yes, yes, yes.*"

Snitch closed his eyes again, then reopened them and after doing this several times realised it was not a dream at all and he was still in the Granite Vault lying on the cold hard floor. The High Minister had vanished and Bysidian Black was now stood by the door on guard.

"What happened?" he moaned rubbing his sore head and standing up.

"You fainted when Fitz said YES" answered Noggin rushing up to Snitch.

"We're going on an adventure Snitch, we're going to find the missing pearl."

"Ohhhh blimey I need air" moaned Snitch stumbling towards the twisted vault door and brushing past Bysidian on the way out. Swiftly following was Noggin who was on the brink of exploding at any moment with excitement. As the chaos left the room and it went quiet again Fitz approached Bysidian.

"Solomon Fear could have taken the pearl absolutely anywhere by now, how are we supposed to find it?"

Checking the corridor outside was clear Bysidian pulled off one of his gloves and produce a small piece of tattered torn paper, wrapped in what looked like the remains of a dirty old coat pocket. "In the fight to stop them I grabbed this," he said pushing it into Fitz's hand. "Now hurry my Warriors will be growing weak and Solomon could open that pearl at any moment. Never trust him do you hear me?"

Looking into the dark towards the Nightmare vault Fitz felt the cold air blow on his face as he tightened his grasp on the rough scrap of paper and cloth. With a deep breath and a last glance at Bysidian Black, he ran out of the vault.

Ember had returned to her platform and was waiting patiently, sat beside her were Snitch and Noggin.

"Okay boss, where do we start?" asked Noggin.

Fitz walked over and sitting down beside them, he unclenched his hand and opened the screwed up piece of paper slamming it on the floor.

"We start here."

Chapter 9

Hidden Messages

It was not very big, badly crinkled up and most of it was missing, presumably still in the pirate's pocket it was ripped from. After a brief moment of looking at the scrap of paper, a confused Snitch asked without even raising his head "Is it just me or is that piece of paper completely blank?"

"It can't be that's not right" replied a flustered Noggin, as she picked up the paper and held it up so the light shone through, turning it over and over to make sure nothing was written on the other side.

Fitz slowly reached out and carefully took the paper back from Noggin's hand. He calmly placed it back on the floor between them and rubbed it with his fingers to try and smooth it out a little.

"Think" whispered Fitz to himself tapping his forehead whilst staring at the paper. "This is Solomon Fear and his pirates, why would one be carrying this if it were not important? It's there, something has to be there, we're just not seeing it." Leaning over the paper to get a closer look he scratched his head and squinted his eyes slightly hoping it might help.

Leaning over Noggin and Snitch joined him until all three were staring closely at the scrap hoping to magically see something hidden there. Snitch slipped off a glove and ran his bare fingertips across the papers surface just in case he could feel something.

As all three stared at the blank piece of paper a warm breeze suddenly started to blow gently on the back of their heads. The breeze wafted their hair, then it stopped for a second and then started again. Stop... start... stop... start... stop...start...

Snitch looked towards a curious Ember who was now leaning over them with her warm breath causing the breeze. She wanted to know what they were all looking at in the tiny huddle on the floor.

"Hey girl," Noggin said still staring at the paper. "Any bright ideas because we are out of them?" Ember leaned in a little closer.

"Careful," said Snitch, "not to close your breath is very warm and if I may say a little smelly" as he rubbed the top of his hot head and scrunched up his nose. Replacing his glove Snitch sat back a little to escape the dragon heat. Fitz's eyes widened in amazement as there suddenly very faint markings started to appear on the scrap of paper.

"THERE" cried Fitz pointing at the paper. "Look right there, it's a map." Ember pulled back startled and the images disappeared again. "No, no, no slowly girl," he said looking into her eyes with, one hand up towards her face to reassure her. "Right here Ember," he said pointing back at the paper.

Ember leaned over again and took a deep breath then gently breathed out a waft of warm air across the paper causing it to flutter on the floor where it lay. As all three looked on the paper slowly revealed the images hidden within.

Let the adventure begin....

Chapter 10

Your Majesty

The cold and crisp autumn night air rushed past their faces making their noses and ears to turn red and tingle from the cold. All three were grateful for the warm radiating glow from Embers fiery scales where they sat. Dream Dragon was certainly the fastest way to travel but not always the warmest as Snitch had declared several times already.

With the stars rushing by like a blur they passed through thick damp clouds which made Fitz close his eyes and repeat the clues drawn on the map over and over to himself. The scrap of map showed London and upon it scrawled haphazardly in black jagged ink were images.

A large bell

A boat

The number 9

A large black feather

A large old looking key

At least they had a starting point London, but what did all the other clues mean? Fitz had no idea but with the Guardians and Bysidian Blacks team of Night Warriors depending on them he knew they needed to figure it out as fast as possible.

Ember started to drop through the clouds until there below them was a sea of twinkling bright lights as the city of London shone out below. Down and down she flew until they were soaring over the rooftops so closely, they were almost able to touch them.

"Look for somewhere safe to land girl" called out Noggin, with her red hair blowing around whipping her stinging cold ears and her nose so red from the cold. Finally, Ember spotted somewhere that she felt looked safe, a large beautiful garden with lots of big trees whose leaves were just turning red and yellow like her scales. There were magnificent bubbling fountains, long winding pathways and delicate roses. At the end stood a set of mighty stone steps sweeping down from a very large house to a lush green lawn.

Landing silently on the grass, away from the house and under cover of the trees, the Dream Drifters slid cautiously from their saddles.

"I think I may have lost my bottom somewhere on the way" groaned Snitch, rubbing his bottom that was numb from the long flight.

"*Shush*" whispered Noggin, "do you hear that?"

In front of them across the long lawn stood the big house, a few lights were on in windows, but one was slightly ajar and raised voices could be heard coming from it.

Slowly and cautiously so as not to be seen the team, followed by Ember, started moving down the path and out across the vast lawn towards the house and the open window. Arriving at the bottom of the grand sweeping steps Fitz strained his neck upwards looking at the tall wall of stone before them.

"I know you're tired, but we need a lift girl." Ember nodded and crouched down for the team to climb aboard. Flying up the steps Ember wobbled a little, it had been a long flight and she felt so desperately tired, but the team needed her, and she was not going to let them down.

With a quick check that the coast was clear Fitz, Noggin and Snitch made a dash for the safety of the house walls only stopping when they reached an area of shadow below the open window.

Fitz looked up at the large stone window sill way above them then at Noggin, who was already holding in her hands the grappling gun from her utility belt.

Aiming it upwards with a tight grip she fired, then giving it a quick tug to make sure it was safe allowed the other two to start climbing. It was a long way but finally, with aching arms and legs, they reached the top. On seeing they were safe Noggin pressed a button on the gun and holding tightly with both hands she rose into the air being pulled upwards to join her friends.

Ember took a moment gathering up every last piece of energy she had to follow them, she was so exhausted. Slipping inside the open window they crouched behind the heavy pink and gold curtains listening to the voices inside.

"What are we going to do Mable?" said one.

"I don't know Alice, I simply don't know what to do" replied a very flustered Mable sounding worried. "She must sleep, or she'll get ill and she is being so mean all of a sudden. We had just better hurry and leave. I have had just about enough of being shouted at today."

Fitz, Noggin and Snitch moved carefully to peep around the heavy curtains and gasped as before them lay a very grand room indeed. The polished wooden floors were covered in large thick pink and gold patterned rugs, on the walls hung beautiful paintings and gold framed mirrors. To one side stood a huge wooden carved bed with the biggest, whitest, comfiest looking pillows Noggin had ever seen. Behind the bed head was a large pink curtain with long golden silk tassels that reached up to a golden crown canopy. There were large comfortable pink sofas and chairs with big feathery soft cushions and a fluffy dog bed all arranged around a large marble fireplace where a roaring fire crackled and popped.

In the centre of the ceiling hung a dazzling crystal chandelier making dancing rainbows around the walls, whilst smaller lamps all around gave the room a cosy glow. Various tables were covered in family photos in golden frames and the air was filled with the sweet scent of fresh roses in vases.

Two ladies dressed in black with white aprons were rushing around turning down the bedcovers, stoking the fire, leaving hot tea on a tray by the sofa and laying fresh thick towels on the bed. Hurrying in their work they left the room by a small side door just in time as within a moment the large double doors at the other end of the room opened and in walked someone, they all recognised instantly.

"Your majesty" whispered Snitch with a gasp. "That's the Queen, the Queen of England. *Blimey,* we must have landed in Buckingham Palace."

The Queen was dressed for bed in a pink soft dressing gown and warm fluffy slippers, her eyes were heavy with exhaustion. Walking across the room slowly she sat down with a huge sigh in one of the sofas by the fire.

"I just do not understand it," she said rubbing behind the ear of one of the corgis that had followed her into the room and was now curled up beside her. "Why whenever I close my eyes can I not sleep properly, I am so, so tired. How can I perform my duties if I can't stay awake and why are there only 2 towels and not three and no sugar with my tea, those silly women?" she snapped.

The corgi looked at her as if listening to every word and then hopped off the sofa before climbing into its own snuggly bed by the fire and drifting off to sleep. Fitz, Noggin and Snitch slowly crept from behind the curtain and back through the open window to the sill outside.

"Hang on, where's Ember, she was right here?" asked Noggin looking around then down to the floor outside.

"Oh no look," said Snitch pointing back into the room. There cuddled up with the corgi in its bed by the fire was Ember. She was curled up in a tiny red ball her scaly tail wrapped around her snoring and looking very cosy indeed. As she was so small the corgi did not mind sharing and the Queen it seemed had not noticed her as she was busy drinking her tea.

"Leave her, let her rest," said Fitz. She will need her energy to get us home again when the time comes."

Chapter 11

Listen

"So, what now?" asked Noggin looking to Fitz for guidance, as he was the team leader after all.

Fitz thought for a second. "We need to go up," he said pointing up the building towards the roof. "Higher, so I can see where we are and further across London."

"Yes sir" replied Noggin, and with that, she grabbed the trusty grappling gun again and shot the line way up to the roof.

Slowly Fitz and Snitch climbed up and up past rows of closed windows, past the magnificent rooms beyond and finally to the top of the palace followed by Noggin.

Running across the never ending roof they finally reached the front of the building. Clambering to the edge they stood in awe looking out across the sea of lights before them.

With the flag on the pole rattling in the night breeze next to him, Snitch clapped his gloved hands together. Like miniature lightning bolts, tiny crackles of sparkling light appeared firstly in his glasses frames and then in black fabric of his gloves. The lights shot down Snitch's fingers to the tips and, as Snitch turned his fingers downwards in front of him, floating in mid-air appeared a keyboard made completely of light.

Tapping away so fast his fingers seemed to blur Snitch searched through the Guardian's vast library for help. All the information was scrolling across the inside of Snitch's glasses in front of his eyes like a large computer screen where only he could see it.

"Ah ha, here it is," he said as his fingers stopped and he pressed a key, causing one of the crackling lights to shine a beam from his glasses frame just above his nose. There, projected on the tall brick chimney breast in front of them was a map of London.

"So, we're here," said Snitch putting his finger in the beam to point at the palace on the map. Pointing in various directions across the roof he continued, "making that way Westminster Abby, that way is Marble Arch and in front of us is St James's Park and that's a giant statue of a pigeon…" Snitch stopped with a confused frown.

"DO YOU MIND?" came the loud voice as the pigeon statue got larger and larger casting a big black shadow across the map. "SOME OF US ARE TRYING TO SLEEP."

Snitch clapped his hands together quickly, causing the gloves and glasses to return to black and the map and keyboard to disappear.

"It's still there" he whispered out of the corner of his mouth towards Noggin who was staring at the half asleep plump grey pigeon waddling towards them.

"Of course, I'm still here I'm not a ghost you know, and I *was* trying to sleep before you rudely interrupted me." The pigeon stopped and looked down at the three tiny Dream Drifters through his sleepy eyes.

"Well, I never saw anything like you before, tiny people on Buckingham Palace roof with magic lights and pictures… Yep I knew it I'm dreaming; I'm going back to bed now it's late," he said turning and starting to waddle away sleepily. "Listen its twelve-o-clock" he slurred pointing a wing across the roof as he fluffed up his feathers and settled back down to sleep.

"LISTEN" shouted Fitz running right to the very roof edge and pointing into the distance in the direction the sound was coming from. *BONG…*

BONG... BONG .... a bell was chiming the hour.

"That's what I said... listen" mumbled the sleepy pigeon. "Darn thing keeps me awake all night noisy thing four times every hour all over London bong, bong, bong and now those people downstairs making a kerfuffle all night, how's a bird supposed to get some shut eye?" His voice drifted off as he started to snore loudly.

"A big bell, a big bell, A BIG BELL" shouted Noggin at Fitz. "It's the next clue."

"It's annoying that's what it is," said the pigeon between his snores.

Clap. The map shone out again. Snitch looked in the direction of the sound and then at the map, tracing with his finger. "Big Ben, its Big Ben, *of course*." The bell stopped on the toll of twelve and Noggin sighed in disappointment.

"It's so far and not one of my gadgets can help us cover that ground quickly," she said searching her belt.

Hopping off the roof ledge he had been stood on Fitz landed next to Noggin with a thud. "Oh, we don't need gadgets," he said smiling as he strolled past her determinedly and across the roof.

The sleeping pigeon had a funny feeling he was being watched. Slowly opening his eyes there before him were three tiny faces staring at him, inches away from his beak. With a startled jump he flapped his wings and fluffed his feathers as he stumbled backwards, falling over his own feet and sitting down with a bump his tail feathers all stuck up in the air.

"Are you okay, we didn't mean to startle you?" asked Noggin rushing towards the bird.

"Whoa wait, your *real* little people?" he said in shock.

"Yes, very real, and we need your help," said Noggin.

Chapter 12

Fat Larry

"This Solomon Fear sounds like a real evil bag of bones," said the pigeon after Fitz, Noggin and Snitch had filled him in on the whole story. "Well, Fat Larry's the name," he said standing up proudly on his pink legs. His white collar and yellow beak shone in the moonlight and he stuck out his purple feathered chest in pride followed by a bow and a swish of his wing. "At your service."

"HOORAY!" cheered Noggin "welcome to the team, we need a ride please."

Now having only ridden on a sleek sharp Dream Dragon with a saddle before, riding on a large plump soft pigeon with no saddle and slippery feathers was a totally new experience for the Dream

Drifters. After managing to clumsily climb around Fat Larry's rather large tummy and hanging onto his feathers to pull themselves onto his back, staying there proved to be not so easy. All they could do was dig their hands and feet far under the feathers and hold on tight.

Fat Larry hopped up onto the roof ledge and looked down at the cobbled courtyard and large gates below. "HOLD TIGHT" he hollered stepping off the edge and proceeding to drop like a stone as he raced towards the ground causing Snitch to scream so high, he almost fainted. Seconds before they hit the ground, he spread open his wings and swooping upwards like a roller coaster. They soared over the big black and gold iron gates at the front of Buckingham Palace and landed on top of a large statue just beyond.

"Evening your majesty" Larry puffed nodding his head at the statue of Queen Victoria who's head he was now clumsily perched on.

"What's wrong?" asked Noggin a little confused at the early landing.

"Sorry, just catching my breath" puffed Fat Larry like a steam train. "Phew, that's exhausting I'm not used to flying so far as there is plenty of food around here from tourists. They don't call me Fat Larry for nothing you know" he said winking at Noggin who giggled.

After a moment's rest, they took off again, this time flying fast and low across the roads as they narrowly missed an oncoming taxi who honked his horn at them. Onwards towards the park, gliding across the damp grass and up above the green, gold and red coloured trees of the park with their leaves starting to fall around them. Swooping across the moonlight shimmering lake their reflection danced back at them in the dark water until they flew out of the other side and onwards into the mighty city.

They climbed above the buildings, growing closer and closer with every wing beat was the tower bathed in light, the mighty clock tower of Big Ben, standing tall and proud. The huge bright clock face glowed white like the moon above.

"GOING UP, HOLD ON TIGHT… *OUCH SNITCH, NOT THAT TIGHT*" cried Fat Larry as he beat his wings with all his might. Up and up they reached the top before gliding around the clock tower and coming to land on a narrow ledge, just in front of the clock face itself.

With a rather undignified wobble Fat Larry sat down with a bump, totally exhausted, causing the unprepared Dream Drifters to lose their grip on his feathers and slide off landing in a pile on the floor. "Oops sorry" he puffed.

Fitz, Noggin and Snitch untangled themselves and brushing the dust off himself Fitz reached inside his backpack taking out the scrap of paper.

"Big Bell… check" he said drawing an imaginary tick through the bell drawn on the map.

"Ok Solomon Fear what's next?" demanded Noggin snatching the piece of map and holding it up ready to go.

"A boat" came the reply from Snitch whose face was a lovely shade of pea green from the flight. "The next clue was a boat and I believe this is yours," he said a little embarrassed holding out a large grey feather towards a less than pleased Fat Larry.

Noggin handed the map back to Fitz who put it safely away. "I didn't see a boat" replied Noggin looking back in the direction they had come from. "I saw trees and water and fountains but no boats, Snitch did you see anything, you were at the back?"

"You mean you had your eyes *open*?" exclaimed a shocked Snitch. "I didn't see anything I was too busy holding on tight and keeping my eyes squeezed shut thank you very much." Fitz and Noggin looked at each other shaking their heads.

"Think, think, think," said Fitz to himself quietly, gently tapping his head. "I can't think with that noise, what is that noise?" he asked looking in the opposite direction.

Fat Larry had done his duty as promised and was now snoring so loudly it sounded more like a monster than a pigeon.

Fitz walked further around the clock ledge and disappeared around the corner out of view, away from the noise to clear his mind leaving Noggin with Snitch. Clap. Snitch started tapping away, his eyes darting back and forth as he read the information scrolling before him.

"Well, come on what does it say?" asked Noggin impatiently as she stretched to try and look over his shoulder hoping to read through the lenses herself.

"*Shush*, will you?" hissed Snitch "I'm trying to read" brushing her away. Noggin moved away with a huff and continued watching Snitch his eyes scrolling through the information. "334 steps to the top, completed in 1859, each side of the tower is 12 meters wide, the four clock dials are made from 312 pieces of opal glass and are 7 meters in diameter" he mumbled to himself.

Suddenly his eyes stopped moving and fixed straight ahead wide open, Snitch stood up so fast that he almost fell off the ledge.

Chapter 13

A Rope of Light

"The wrong side" whispered Snitch in disbelief to himself.

"What do you mean?" Noggin looked at him with her face screwed up in confusion.

"*FOUR* clock dials, don't you see? We're on the …."

"WRONG SIDE" the sentence was finished by a shout from Fitz who they could no longer see. "HERE, IT'S HERE" he shouted.

Noggin and Snitch turned towards the shout running carefully along the ledge and trying not to look down, around the corner they went until they came across Fitz standing looking out from the tower.

"Boats, lots of boats, look," said Fitz pointing below. There below them was the wide river with boats of every size bobbing up and down in every direction, some moving and some moored for the night.

"WAHOO!" shouted Noggin as she jumped up and punched the air so close to the edge that Snitch had to grab her utility belt to keep her safe.

"So, all we need to do now is get down there," said Snitch poking his nose out over the edge and quickly regretting it. His knees went weak and wobbly and goose bumps shot up all over him in fear as he stumbled backwards to stand close against the wall behind him.

Fitz grinned smugly. "No problem we have a ride remember?" as he started to walk away back along the ledge towards the snoring pigeon.

At this very moment, there was a loud clonk from inside the tower as the big hand on the clock face dropped and came to rest on the number 6.

"OH, NO" screamed Snitch with terror in his eyes. "HOLD ON RIGHT NOW" he yelled after Fitz as he grabbed Noggin's arm and dragged her down with him to their knees balancing on the ledge.

The clock tower shook as the deafening half past the hour chimes rung out across London, causing the Dream Drifters to hang on for their lives.

BONG... BONG... BONG....

With the gigantic bell ringing in his ears so loudly it felt like the whole world shook Fitz looked up to see the feathery panic that was Fat Larry flying away at high speed. He was heading back towards the safety of his home at Buckingham Palace no doubt. Fitz dropped his head in disappointment and waited for the noise to stop.

"Everyone ok?" he called back to see Snitch and Noggin nodding still holding their ears. "Well, there goes our ride" as he watched Fat Larry disappearing into the distance. "Noggin it's over to you and your gadgets now, any ideas?"

Noggin looked at her belt. "Snitch how far is it to the ground?" she asked rummaging around in all her pockets and the items hanging from her belt.

Clap. Snitch removed his sparkling glasses and holding them carefully in an outstretched arm shuffled forwards slightly and held them out over the tower edge. His eyes were tight shut just in case he could see down, his knees were shaking, and he had a horrible tight feeling in his tummy as the glasses beamed several thin rays of lights down the tower and to the floor way below.

"I thought you were supposed to wear them when you did that?" grinned Fitz looking at Snitch's eyes which looked so tiny without them on.

"If you think I'm going to wear them and then stand and look over the edge to the floor you must be *crazy*" replied Snitch stepping back to the wall and putting the glasses back on to read the numbers they had projected back. "54.9 meters that's about 16 stories so basically a *really, really, really, really* long way down".

Noggin shook her head. "Too far for the grappling gun or a rope," she said and paused for a second before a thought came to mind. "I do have another option," she said pulling from her belt an item Fitz had not seen before.

In Noggins hand lay a black disk that at first Fitz though maybe an ice hockey puck. He watched as Noggin threw it against the stonewall behind them and it stuck with a thud just below the clock face.

"It's something I've been working on with the Guardians in their workshop," she said. "We've not had chance to test it fully, but we only get one shot at it," she said looking at Fitz for his agreement to continue.

"I trust you" replied Fitz confidently nodding and glancing sideways sharply at Snitch who was slowly raising his hand to speak. Without a sound gradually Snitch put his hand back down realising this was not the moment to mention the utter terror that was bouncing around in his stomach.

Walking to the very edge of the ledge Noggin looked down making Snitch shiver.

"Ah yes there that will do nicely" she declared. From one of her many pockets, she took out something that looked like a black pen. With it firmly in her grip, she twisted the end and a red laser, so bright it made Snitch look away, shone out beaming way down into the streets below. Expertly moving the pen Noggin guided the red beam until it shone like a small red dot on top of a streetlight overhanging the river.

"Stand back" she warned looking in turn at the inquisitive Fitz and Snitch to make sure they were clear.

With a press of her thumb, she clicked a button on the end and like a bullet from a gun a beam of light shot from the centre of the black disk on the wall down to the streetlight Noggin had selected below, creating a line of dazzling light.

"Wow" mouthed Snitch but no sound came out.

Noggin glanced at her two team members partly in pride and partly in utter surprise, it had worked.

"Now what?" asked Fitz excitedly wanting to see more.

"Now, we need these" replied Noggin as she handed a pair of small round metal bracelets to the puzzled pair. "Put them on, one on each wrist and make sure they close tightly. I'll go first" she instructed.

Fitz had his mouth open, just about to question Noggin on their use when she threw her hands up above her head with one either side of the rope of light she was standing under. With a crackle, a beam of white light appeared between the two bracelets connecting them above the light rope.

 "A zip line, that's amazing" exclaimed Fitz in delight as he realised what Noggin was planning. Noggin grinned proudly.

Taking a deep breath, she stepped off the ledge into thin air, zooming down the light rope at high speed until just above the streetlight the beam broke between her bracelets and she landed with a thump on the top. It was such a long way down that Snitch and Fitz could only just see her.

With a wave to show she was safe Fitz turned to Snitch "your turn" he said but Snitch didn't move.

"Maybe you go first" stammered a shaking Snitch but Fitz was not silly, he knew if he went there was no way Snitch would ever follow him and then what would they do?

"Snitch please," said Fitz his voice calm and reassuring. "I need you to go first so I know both of my team are safe. I understand you're scared, I am as well but it's the only way down and we have to keep moving or it will be daylight before we know it. Please Snitch trust me I would never let anything bad happen to you I promise."

Snitch knew Fitz was right he could feel it deep down inside, but his head was telling him to panic. He had to calm himself and believe in the trust he had for his teammates, so after a few deep breaths slowly he made his way to the light rope. Fitz knelt down locking his hands together like a step and slowly a very scared and shaky Snitch placed a foot in Fitz's hands lifting himself up to reach the above beam of light.

Fitz nodded at him proudly as Snitch raised his shaking hands and his bracelets lit up, his knees were knocking and then he made the big mistake of looking down.

"ARRRRRGGHHHHH!" he cried "I really think…." But he was too late as Fitz had no choice and gave him a push just enough to send him off the edge and shooting down the light rope.

With his legs flapping around as if he was dancing on ice and his eyes so tightly shut, they stung, all Snitch could do was hold on and scream very, very loudly. Noggin caught him when he landed as a terrified Snitch grabbed her for a huge hug, holding on and not wanting to let go.

"Snitch open your eyes," she said holding his shaking body. "You're here, your safe, I've got you. I am so proud of you."

Slowly opening his tear filled eyes Snitch realising he was hugging Noggin so tightly she might pop so he released his grip and sat down trying to catch his breath.

"That has to be the worst thing you have ever, ever asked me to do," he said. "I will never ever, ever complain about flying Dream Dragon again I promise." Noggin smiled and turned to wave both hands at Fitz letting him know the coast was clear for him to join them.

With all three safely on the streetlight, Noggin pressed the pen button again and the rope of light disappeared. Sighing she packed the three pairs of tiny bracelets into her pocket. "One use, only for now but we're working on it," she said proudly looking back up at the black disk that remained forever on the clock tower above.

To their side a stone arched bridge spanned across the water and across the river they could see a giant wheel lit in all colours, stretching high into the sky as it cast a shimmering reflection on the fast flowing river below. The sound of water lapping against the brick walls under the streetlight became louder and louder as a boat passed by causing large rippling waves to crash against the walls. Boats of all shapes and sizes were slowly travelling in both directions along the river with Fitz watching them curiously.

"Which boat, which way?" he repeated to himself, almost as if he were hoping by magic Solomon Fear's voice would be heard telling him the answer.

Snitch sat huddled tight holding his knees on the warm light, Fitz could see he had stopped shaking now but he needed a moment to recover. Noggin, however, had no such fear; she was stood on tiptoe leaning right out across the dark murky water below and looking to the right down the river.

With no warning in a rush of panic, she scrabbled for her night vision goggles and quickly put them on. There in the distance bobbing towards them was a boat with a flag on the back.

"PIRATES!!!" yelled Noggin whizzing off her goggles and jumping back.

Chapter 14

A Big Trampoline

Snitch shot up in terror, Fitz ran to where Noggin had stood and looked out squinting into the dark beyond, there was no time to reach for his night vision goggles as the boat was almost upon them. With its noisy engine chugging the boat moved closer and closer until Fitz could make its shape out from the shadows.

It was big and wide with row upon row of seats, some inside a glass area and some outside in the open air. They were all covered with a large white canopy roof, almost like a sail, stretched tightly above them. With only a few lights on it was hard to see properly but at the back, moving in the night breeze Noggin was right there waved a pirate's flag.

It was big and black with the white skull and crossbones rippling in the cold night air.

"SNITCH" yelled Fitz at which point Snitch forgot all his fear and jumped into action. Clap. Looking out towards the ship Snitch started to scan with his glasses the object moving towards them. The keyboard burst into life, his fingers tapping away so fast they were again a blur whilst his glasses continued to scan the approaching ship.

On one half of his glasses appeared an image showing the boat moving towards them, including the face of the driver at the back. On the other half appeared an image of Solomon Fears Pirate ship 'The Swirling Pearl'.

"It's not them," said Snitch in relief. "The Guardians database says it's called a tourist boat. Apparently visiting people use it to see the city and the sights from the water, it must be moving along the river ready for use tomorrow."

"Phew, that was close" puffed Fitz.

"Wasn't the next clue a boat?" interrupted Noggin hurriedly looking at them both. Fitz and Snitch nodded in reply. "Well, if there was ever a clue for which boat it is from all the other boats out there" waving her arm towards the river, "then this has to be it and we need to get on *that* boat and quickly" pointed Noggin.

Fitz looked at her and in an instant realised, as she had, that there was only one way to do that as the boat was now starting to pass under the streetlight and they were about to lose their chance.

Fitz and Noggin ran past Snitch to the very back of the streetlight leaving Snitch bemused for a second. Then as they turned to face him swiftly the realisation of what they were about to do struck him.

"FITZ, NOGGIN, NOOOOO ARRGGHH!!!" he yelled in terror waving his hands frantically around as they both ran towards him at lightning speed. With one either side, they scooped him up under the arms, lifted his feet off the floor and threw themselves and poor Snitch off the end of the streetlight.

With the sound of Big Ben ringing out above them the three landed on the boat roof with an almighty bounce, just like landing on a big trampoline.

Snitch was now going simply crazy. Arms and legs were flying around, and his burning red angry face looked like a big juicy tomato covered in white spiky hair.

"What was that, sorry I can't hear you?" pretended Noggin, as she cupped her hand to her ear whilst trying to hide a smile very unsuccessfully.

"Is he supposed to be that colour?" joked Fitz.

"…AND THAT'S ALL I HAVE TO SAY TO YOU TWO" screamed Snitch his hands clenched in fists waving at them just as Big Ben fell silent.

With his face still screwed up in anger and totally exhausted from his outburst he promptly walked a distance away from the others. Laying down on his back he watched the passing night sky and wondered which of the stars was home. The air was getting colder and the boat was rocking slowly side to side in the water. The deep chugging of the engine made Snitch start to relax and he began to feel sleepy.

As they started to move gradually further out into the centre of the river Fitz decided this was a good time to look at the clues again and try to figure out their next move. Sitting with Noggin he reached inside his backpack and took out the scrap of paper.

"Number 9 well, that could be anything," he said glancing sideward at Noggin.

As they passed under a bridge the air quickly went very cold and dark chilling Fitz to the bone and reminding him of the vault of nightmares. He shuddered in the darkness as the engine noise echoed loudly off the stone walls and bridge arches above them. The waves slapped against the mighty brick feet stood in the water until the boat came out the other side and the reassuring lights of the city reappeared.

"1" came the very sleepy voice of Snitch a distance away.

"Oh, so you are still talking to us?" smirked Noggin as her favourite past time was to annoy Snitch who was still staring up to the sky.

"Actually, I'm not talking to you, I'm talking to myself thank you" came the sleepy reply with a yawn and a stretch.

"Well, you carry on smarty pants, but do it quietly will you were doing important things unlike you."

Fitz smiled at his team, they were his best friends and even though they loved to annoy each other, which always made him smile, he knew they would risk everything to protect one another.

"1,2,3" as Noggin started counting pointing at the large wheel lighting up the river.

"Do you see something?" asked Fitz in hope as she continued.

"4,5,6 7 no never mind" her voice trailed off. "There are lots more than 9 glass balls around the outside".

Snitch tutted "They are not glass balls silly, they are carriages where people sit to go around on the big wheel and look out over the city, it's called The London Eye."

"Oh well *excuse me* Mr I know everything," said Noggin waggling her head at him.

As the boat bobbed along the lights of the city reflected in the water. Fitz's mind started to drift back to home, he thought about everything that had happened, the worried look on Bysidian Black and the Guardians faces, and he began to wonder what could lay ahead for him and his team.

"If we find the missing Nightmare Pearl," asked Noggin as if reading his mind "do you think *he* will be there?" Neither of them had ever seen Solomon Fear or any of his pirate crew but they had heard many stories and he was definitely not someone Fitz wanted to cross paths with.

"I'm not sure but if he is, we need to be prepared, and it's *when* Noggin not *if* we find the missing pearl," he said with a confident smile. "We will do this, we're the best team for the job, the High Minister said so, we know we are the best and everyone is depending on us including the team of Night Warriors trapped inside that pearl. We *can*, and we *will* find that pearl" he said with determination.

Noggin smiled and the twinkle in her eye went from fear to excitement. "Well, what are we waiting for" she replied as she jumped up with a bounce. "If we save the day Bysidian Black's bound to want me to become a Night Warrior and be honest we all know I would be absolutely perfect for the job" she declared bouncing around.

"2 and 3" came the sleepy sound of Snitch again but the others were not listening to him.

Standing up Fitz walked with a bounce to the back of the boat roof, he was now standing directly above the boat drivers head with only the roof covering between them, but he was so small the driver had no idea he was even there.

"9,9,9 mmm….9 buildings, no too many to count, 9 boats no, 9 cranes, 9 flag poles, 9 9 9 come on Fitz think," he said crossly to himself, "what can you see that they would see?" The answer was out there somewhere, and Fitz was getting increasingly annoyed as he walked and bounced his way back to join Noggin.

"5" Snitch mumbled.

"IF YOU'RE NOT GOING TO HELP US THEN PLEASE JUST BE QUIET" snapped Fitz.

Noggin stopped jumping around shocked by Fitz's outburst and hurriedly started to look around the roof hanging over the edge, checking her pockets and scrabbling around in Fitz's backpack.

"What *are* you doing?" he said abruptly.

"It's here it has to be here," she said looking around.

"WHAT HAS?" snapped back a confused Fitz.

"The pearl silly listen to your voice, it's just like in the vault," said Noggin staring at Fitz.

Fitz stopped as he realised how he sounded. "It's not here" he promised. "I'm just angry because Solomon Fear is beating us at the moment, and he will not win."

"6" came Snitch's dreamy voice in the middle of the sentence.

The two stopped speaking and turned towards Snitch. "Oh, 6 what?" huffed Noggin with a frown but Snitch ignored her as he was sleepy, comfortable and really did not want her annoying him anymore.

"Snitch what exactly are you counting?"

Chapter 15

The Number 9

"Bridges silly look here comes 7" murmured a sleepy Snitch pointing upwards as they passed under another. "Isn't it lovely? We've passed under 7 now, all shapes and sizes with pretty lights and everything" he said smiling dreamily closing his eyes again.

"Bridges" repeated Fitz jumping up. "Right there in front of our eyes of course," he said quickly turning to Noggin.

"Snitch you are simply *BRILLIANT*!" she replied. Snitch turned his head in surprise as she had never called him brilliant before, ever.

"Are you sure it's 7 already?" questioned Fitz running over to where Snitch lay.

"Yes, definitely 7 and here comes 8," said Snitch getting to his feet and pointing ahead.

Running along the bouncy roof they stopped at the front just as bridge number 8 with its giant arches loomed ahead. As the cold damp air hit their faces, they passed under bridge number 8 slowly, rocking side to side the sounds of the waves echoing on the bridge above their heads. Leaving the shadows under the bridge they came out into the night sky to be faced with the biggest ship they had ever seen, grey and menacing like an iron floating monster against the night sky.

"AARRGGHH!!! PIRATES!"

squealed Snitch hiding behind Fitz.

Noggin and Fitz burst out laughing. "Snitch that is not The Swirling Pearl" they reassured him.

As they sailed around the gigantic warship its huge chains clanking loudly as they hit the metal hull like a drum and all its guns and towering masts stood strong and proud against the night sky. With all their concentration on the warship they were passing none of them had been looking ahead until Snitch suddenly gasped in awe.

"Now *that's* what I call a bridge."

Standing majestically in front of them like a giant gateway across the river was the almighty bridge number 9 with its two colossal towers, lit up like a beacon in the night.

"That's Tower Bridge" explained Snitch reading from the Guardians library, "and that mighty floating beast we just passed was HMS Belfast, wow just imagine if Solomon Fear got his hands on that, not even Bysidian or his team of Night Warriors could ever stop him then" he cringed.

"Well, if that's bridge 9 then we need to get off this boat quickly and I'm sorry to say but it doesn't look like it's stopping to me" exclaimed Noggin.

"Can we use you're grappling gun to hook under the bridge?" suggested Fitz.

"I'm not sure I think we're moving too fast. It's not safe we could be pulled off the boat into the river and I'm not sure it would hold all three of us at once, never mind pull us all up to safety" replied Noggin frantically.

Quickly she checked her belt for another option. "No, no, no," she said quickly going through everything she had the panic rising in her voice. "Oh boy, I feel some time with the Guardians in their workshop to create more gadgets coming on" she muttered to herself. Through his glasses, Snitch started to scan the bridge approaching them now quicker than ever.

"HURRY" he yelled we're going to be under it in 5 seconds,4....3...2...1."

With time gone Noggin had no other option but to trust in the grappling gun. "We're going to have to climb and prey its long enough" she yelled as they started to pass under the centre of the bridge.

Holding the gun with all her might she balanced herself on the rocking boat and fired sending the hook flying towards the metal framework under the bridge. It wound around and hooked onto one of the thick metal beams with a clang. There was a loud Snap as the end of the line shot out of the gun snatching it from Noggins grasp and, in an instant, it disappeared under the murky water below.

"YES," she cried "just long enough" as the line wafted within reach.

The boat was now rocking faster and harder as the water swelled under the giant bridge and the waves rolled back from the bridges sturdy brick feet that sat deep in the water. With a quick tug on the line to make sure it was safe she called back to the others.

"COME ON JUMP." Launching herself off the roof Noggin caught the dangling line climbing up a little, so she could grip it with her legs and arms.

Fitz and Snitch did not need telling twice, they ran for the swinging line but just as they were about to jump an almighty wave hit the boat causing it to rock hard left then right. Losing his balance Snitch staggered side to side before falling hard to his knees, desperately grabbing with his hands he tried to grip onto the slippery roof as he slid towards the edge.

"Hold on I've got you" cried Fitz grabbing his teammate's arm as tightly as he could so he did not roll off the roof into the murky water below. Snitch stumbled back to his feet grabbing Fitz to steady himself.

"*RUN, HURRY, RUN*" yelled Noggin as she swung frantically to and fro on the dangling line, her panic rising as she saw her teammates moved further and further away from her.

"COME ON WE'RE LOSING HER" Fitz cried as the two ran along the roof staggering side to side towards the back of the boat as it rocked against the waves.

"WE'RE NOT GOING TO MAKE IT WE ARE MOVING TO FAST" hollered Snitch his little legs were running as fast as they would go whilst being pulled along by Fitz.

"Oh yes we are, *HOLD ON*" bellowed Fitz as his grip tightened on Snitch's arm and with that, he launched them both up into the air.

They landed with a huge bounce on the tarpaulin roof that was rapidly disappearing as the boat moved under the bridge. Like a giant trampoline, Fitz and Snitch flew high off the roof and stretching out their arms caught the line just as the boat sailed away from under their feet leaving the three dangling in mid-air.

Chapter 16

Move Now

"NOW CLIMB," yelled Noggin. "Come on as fast as you can" as she started to hoist herself up.

Fitz and Snitch started to follow, but the line was dripping wet from the water splashing below, every stretch made their arms and legs ache with pain and their hands were so sore.

"I need to stop for a moment" cried Snitch wrapping his aching feet around the line. "My arms are breaking, it's so cold and I can't feel my fingers as my gloves are wet with freezing river water. I can't hold on, I'M SLIPPING" he screamed leaving Fitz trapped dangling below him.

"HOLD ON, I'M COMING" shouted Noggin who was almost at the top of the line. Releasing her

119

grip, she slid down stopping just above Snitch. "We can do this" she said trying to calm the petrified Snitch. "Come on one hand then the other slowly. I'll stay with you just keep looking at me" as she tried not to focus on the fast flowing river below and not letting Snitch look down.

They started to climb again as a relieved Fitz followed when suddenly, a loud alarm started to sound out from the bridge somewhere above them. They all froze.

"What's that?" asked Snitch with fear all over his face. Noggin looked up but could see nothing but the underside of the bridge.

"I don't know but you can bet it's not good," she said.

"MOVE NOW" came the yell from below. Climbing frantically up the line was Fitz heading towards Snitch who in turn started to climb as fast as he could in panic behind Noggin. The alarm continued to ring in their ears and then a sudden whirring and clanking sound started to come from under the bridge.

"HURRY" yelled Fitz catching Snitch up. "IT'S OPENING, THE BRIDGE IS OPENING."

Sailing towards the bridge along the city lit river was a large boat, too big to fit under it when it was closed so the bridge was opening to let it pass. As the bridge started to open the line started to lift, higher and higher as it swayed harder and harder with the three tiny Dream Drifters hanging on, still climbing for their lives.

"I'M SLIPPING" shrieked Noggin as she slid down towards Snitch, almost sitting on his head who, in turn, started to slide towards Fitz. In a bundle, almost back at the bottom of the line, they all hung on with everything they could as the rivers swirling black water rushed by below.

"HOLD ON, HOLD ON" yelled a terrified Fitz desperately trying to help Snitch and Noggin whilst his own grip slipped.

"I CAN'T, WE'RE GOING TO HIT IT"
shrieked Snitch as the line started to swing like a
trapeze towards one of the huge stone bases of a
tower.

"ARRGGHHHHHHHHHHHHH!!!!"

they screamed the three finally lost their grips and
the end of the line slipped through their fingers.

Chapter 17

Feather and Key

Fitz closed his eyes waiting for the cold dark water to engulf him when he felt a sharp jerk followed by a hard tug on his backpack straps. His hair was blown flat against the back of his head by a strong rush of wind and he could feel nothing below his feet. Fitz opened his eyes abruptly and saw the river rushing away from below him. He was flying.

Confused he turned his head to see Noggin who was hanging onto Snitch with both arms as tightly as she could, safe and sound in the tight grasp of Fat Larry.

"As I said, at your service" cooed Fat Larry as he flew up through the gap in the now fully open bridge with Noggin, Snitch and Fitz dangling from his pink knobbly feet. Flying high to the top of the bridge he carefully lowered his three weary and shaking passengers onto the safety of a tower roof and landed next to them.

"Phew, well I don't know about you but I'm *exhausted*. I've been looking for you everywhere, that big bell you found sure is loud. It nearly scared all my feathers off, a naked Fat Larry now that would not be a pretty sight" he chuckled to himself.

"That was *amazing* you saved us" squealed Noggin running over and giving Fat Larry a huge hug with her aching arms.

Fitz smiled. "But I saw you fly away I thought you had gone home."

"Home, oh no" exclaimed Fat Larry. "All that way no, no I just flew away until that awful noise stopped but when I came back you had disappeared. I did look around for you, but I got tired and that great big boat was passing by" he said pointing towards the large boat disappearing up the river.

"So, I hitched a ride and had a little snooze" he cooed. Noggin grinned, she was sure Fat Larry probably spent more time snoozing than he did awake. "Next thing I remember is waking up as the boat slowed down for the bridge to open, I looked up and there you were dangling like worms on a fishing line." Fat Larry glanced over at Snitch who was still lying down with his eyes closed and his legs wobbling. "I'm guessing that wasn't part of the plan?"

Fitz shook his head "I don't think we really have a plan but one thing's for sure I'm glad we have you on the team, thank you."

"That goes for me too," said Snitch who sat up to join his team mates looking sadly at his wet gloves.

"Oh, now look you've made me blush," said Fat Larry nudging Snitch and winking. "Here put those wet gloves in here," he said fluffing up his feather's, so he looked twice the size. "They will soon dry" as Snitch carefully placed the gloves beneath a big fluffy warm grey feather. "Oh, they are really cold" shivered Fat Larry chuckling.

In the distance chimes of Big Ben rang out, it seemed such a long way away from where they were sat right now but home seemed much further. Noggin looked up at the sky, but the stars didn't seem to twinkle as brightly as usual.

"It's the lights of the city" explained Snitch. "They stop us from seeing all the stars as clearly as we do at home."

"They sure are beautiful though" whispered Noggin as she looked out before them at the city in all its glory, lights in all colours shone into to the sky, reflecting on other buildings windows and making the river sparkle as far as they could see.

One building, in particular, had caught Fitz's eye. "What's that building, it looks very old like a fortress or a castle or something?" asked Fitz.

"Oh, that's a beauty isn't it and one of my personal favourites. It's very, very old" said Fat Larry. "That is the Tower".

"The Tower?" questioned Snitch.

"Yes, The Tower of London" continued Fat Larry. "Of course, we don't go in their due to those mean Ravens that live inside. They don't like us pigeons, they chase us and say we're not important like them all high and mighty la de da they are."

"How dare they" chirped Noggin. "You're a hero and very important indeed, especially to us anyway …. Err what's a raven anyway?"

"Oh, they are big black mean ugly looking birds with sharp beaks, big wings, claws and evil beady black eyes. They live in there guarding the tower and the jewels and they never leave, so we stay out here, and they live in there and everyone's happy" shrugged Fat Larry.

"Mean, ugly, sharp beaks and beady evil eyes?" repeated Snitch looking scared. "Well I'm glad they're in there and we are out here," he said with a gulp.

"Hang on just one second, jewels? There are jewels inside?" Noggin asked pointing at the tower.

"Yep, that's where The Queen keeps all her Crown Jewels and all those sparkly things she has under lock and key, so they are safe" replied Fat Larry as he handed Snitch back his now super warm and dry gloves. "I don't understand it personally, I mean if you can't eat them then what's so important about them?"

Fitz had been quiet till now listening to the conversation when suddenly it all became clear. "*Of course*," he cried, and, in an instant, pulled out the scrap of map waving it at the others. "It's in there," he said pointing at the Tower "it's in there. Look, the last two pictures, a big black feather and a big key, it's in there Solomon's hidden the pearl in there." Snitch, Noggin and Fat Larry stopped speaking. "Where better to hide a pearl than among crowns and treasures that are covered in them?" asked Fitz.

"Oh, very crafty" whispered Fat Larry nodding his head.

"*Of course,* how clever you are Solomon Fear" cried Noggin "but we're hot on your heels and were coming so you'd better run."

Chapter 18

The Oddest Feeling

Fat Larry landed quietly on the leaf covered grass in the shadow of a large tree between the outer and inner walls of the Tower. This was as far as he could take them as the Ravens lived beyond.

"Be safe little friends" he cooed as Fitz, Noggin and Snitch slid off his back carefully. They watched as he flew away, over the wall aiming back along the river bank towards Buckingham Palace, with a snooze or two on the way no doubt. They all felt a little sad to see him go.

"So, team how do we get in here?" asked Fitz, looking at the tall thick walls with closed wooden gates before him.

Having scanned the immediate area for openings and had no luck, Snitch started to examine a plan of the Tower and its grounds he had found in the Guardians Library. "There are not many ways in, but then again it is a fortress, the only way I can see is if we use the drains. Look there is a cover here we could climb...."

"DRAINS? *Pooeeyyy* no way" interrupted Noggin "I have a better idea" as she pushed a loose brick out of the bottom of the wall. "How about we go this way?" she said pointing smugly.

"Now who's the smarty pants?" asked Snitch.

As Noggin and Snitch climbed through the tiny gap in the wall Fitz stopped. The hairs on his neck were standing up and he had the oddest feeling they were being watched. Looking around he couldn't see anyone, yet still, the feeling would not go away. Something was not right, examining the loose stone he noticed the mortar was all dust on the floor looking like it had been scraped away not simply fallen out. That stone had not come loose without some help and Fitz knew exactly who had helped it.

Once inside they moved quickly along the edge of the wall, keeping to the shadows, finding a bench to hide under where it felt safe to stop and plan their next move.

"Snitch we need to locate which of the buildings the Crown Jewels are in and how to get there the quickest way possible" instructed Fitz taking charge. Snitch clapped his palms together as quietly as possible and started typing away whilst Fitz slowly looked around. Most of the open area was lit but it was the shadows he was more concerned about.

Moving slightly away from the others Fitz discreetly slipped on his night vision goggles so as not to alarm them and examined the shadows for any sign of movement. They were here he could feel them.

"Got it," said Snitch as he pressed his hands together making the keyboard disappear. "It's that building over there," he said pointing into the distance.

Fitz removed his goggles in haste and clipped them back on his belt, hoping they had not seen but as he turned, he saw Noggin and Snitch looking at him with concern.

"They're, here aren't they?" asked Noggin with a wobble of fear in her voice as she looked around.

Fitz had not wanted to alarm his team but nodded. "Yes, but I can't see them yet, they're hiding just watching us I can feel them."

"Maybe I can help," said Snitch moving in front of the other two to get a clear view from beneath the bench. With his glasses he scanned the vast open area between them and the Jewel House moving his head from left to right and up and down.

"No, I can't see anyone either" he sighed and went to clap his hands. "Wait a second" he stopped as something moving in the distance caught his eye. "Yes, 1-2-3-4 over there just coming out of the Jewel House, but they are not watching us, in fact, I don't think they know were here. They seem awfully busy trying to carry a big chest."

"Can you see what's inside?" asked Noggin reaching for her night vision goggles to take a look.

"No, the lids closed" Snitch replied, "but it looks really, really heavy." As Snitch watched the four pirates lifted the chest, two at either end and started to walk away from the Jewel House along the path. With his finger pressed firmly on his lips for them to not make a sound Snitch silently pushed Fitz and Noggin back into the darkest shadows behind them.

The four pirates passed them by so closely, they could almost hear them breathing. Clumsily they pushed the heavy chest through the gap in the wall then one by one disappeared after it.

"Stay here" instructed Fitz firmly running towards the gap. He stopped at its side with his heart thumping in his chest before peeping through and then following.

Chapter 19

Off with their Heads

The scruffy pirates ran closely along the bottom of the wall, banging their legs with the heavy chest. "Hurry up," said one in a gruff voice.

"Don't rush me this thing is heavy" snapped another as they stumbled around the corner out of sight.

Fitz followed but running around the corner he skidded to an abrupt halt, hastily running back out of view he peeped around the corner so as not to be seen. There before him floating just above the ground was the pirate's mighty ship with its name emblazoned down the side in silver,

THE SWIRLING PEARL

The evil looking ship had a shining jet-black hull and three tall masts hanging with tattered ropes and ladders, three rows of ragged grey sails on each. The sails billowed in the night breeze as if impatiently waiting to fly the pirates through the night sky.

At the back, a giant wheel that looked like a serpent holding its own tail stood carved in black ebony wood. Guarding the bow, a figurehead of a dragon winged serpent, its mouth stretched wide open with silver fangs and orange eyes glimmering in the streetlights as if keeping watch. From a window, at the back, a low candlelight flickered from the captain's quarters.

The gun deck had row upon row of cannons ready for battle and at the top of each mast flew the large skull and crossbones flags rippling in the breeze as if they were alive, their evil eyes staring straight at Fitz.

"Look alive lads, give us a hand" yelled one as they dragged the heavy trunk onto the bottom of the floating ship's ramp, with that three other pirates appeared from below deck.

"Heave" one cried as they pushed and pulled the heavy chest.

"Come on lads we need to hurry; we should have done this by now and be gone. Fancy having to come back again, those guards frightened the life out me, the Captain almost got caught you know."

"I've always said it's not safe here in daylight," said another shaking his head. "We were that close to being seen," he said holding up his finger and thumb with a tiny gap between them.

"All I can say is lucky the Captain heard them coming and managed to swap it quickly and hide our treasure," said another patting the chest lid. "Can you believe they opened that case and took that crown out with him still in there and they never saw him? That's why *he's* the Captain, fearless he is."

With that, the chest was finally at the top of the ramp. Fitz listened as they puffed and pulled dragging it across the deck, their voices getting quieter and quieter before it went silent as they took the chest below deck.

Noggin and Snitch were still waiting as instructed beneath the bench where he had left them. They were very relieved to see Fitz running back towards them through the gap in the wall.

"What did you see, where did they go?" they asked together eagerly. Fitz caught his breath and quickly filled them in on all he had seen and heard.

"So, Solomon Fear swapped the stolen Nightmare Pearl for a real pearl inside on one of the Queens crowns. Well, you can bet that's what's in the chest, the real pearl" declared Snitch.

"That's going to be like looking for a needle in a haystack" Noggin cried. "There must be hundreds of pearls in there."

Fitz looked out from under the bench, between them and the Jewel House lay a very large open area of grass with pathways and trees. The whole area was lit up by bright lights making him feel very uneasy.

"Ok team we have to get across there, stay together, stay low and move fast," he said looking them both in the eyes to make sure they understood.

Quickly but cautiously they left the safety of the shadows beneath the bench running as fast as they could. Staying low they kept looking all around and above making their way across the grass towards the building. Fitz still had that horrible feeling they were being watched but what was it? The pirates were on the ship, so it couldn't be them.

"Keep moving, come on, stay together we're almost there" Fitz instructed in a stern whisper as he jumped down the neatly trimmed grass edge dropping onto the gravel path below that led directly to the Jewel House.

To us humans we wouldn't even notice it but, to a tiny Dream Drifter, the drop from the grass edge to the path below was deep.

"Careful" he called back, "there's a step here" jumping and landed on both feet followed by Noggin but Snitch wasn't listening as he was too busy trying to keep up. Missing the step, he stumbled and fell flat on his front sending his glasses tumbling to the floor. Instantly Fitz and Noggin were by his side helping him to his feet quickly and picking up his glasses, but as they all turned to carry on running, they slid to a halt. The path ahead was blocked.

"Well, well, well lads look what we have here," said the large black glossy bird standing tall and menacing between them and the building they so needed to get to. Peering at them with cold marble like glistening black eyes it tapped one sharp claw on the hard ground.

"Oh no" whispered Snitch. "Mean, ugly, sharp beaks and evil beady eyes, just as Fat Larry described."

"I told you I wasn't seeing things, didn't I?" the raven said as two more appeared on the path behind them.

"You sure did Cedric" one replied as it leant in towards them and nudged Snitch in the back with his dirty beak.

Noggin, Fitz and Snitch huddled together, standing back to back and breathing faster and faster in fear, not sure which way to look first as they were surrounded by Ravens. Fitz had been right, they were indeed being watched but not by the pirates as he first thought, it was the ravens that had been watching them the whole time.

"What do you think they are?" asked another curiously turning his head sideward and looking at them very closely with one glinting eye.

"I'm not sure, never seen anything like them in all my years Odin," said the other.

"HEY BACK OFF" yelled Noggin bravely running forward and bopping the raven directly in the eyeball with a punch.

"*OUCH*, IT HIT ME" the shocked raven squawked screwing his sore eye up and stepping back as the other ravens just cackled.

"Noggin stop it" shouted Fitz grabbing her and pulling her towards him. "Don't make them angry."

"Hear that boys, they talk, well fancy that" continued the raven they called Cedric. "The question is what are you doing in our tower in the middle of the night?" he demanded moving in closer, causing Noggin, Snitch and Fitz to huddle even closer together. "No one's allowed in here at night, no one. Do you hear me?" he snapped.

"I say their trouble" replied one behind them.

"Yes, trouble indeed" agreed another glaring at them moving closer and closer. "So, Cedric what do we do with them?"

"Well, you know what we do with intruders at the tower don't you" Cedric replied. "Off with their heads."

Chapter 20

Truly Bonkers

"NO, YOU DON'T" yelled Noggin and quick as a flash she pulled the laser pen out of her pocket and shone it directly in Cedric's eyes.

"CAW, CAW, I'm blind" he squawked loudly as he stumbled backwards in pain and surprise, holding his wing across his eyes. "GET THEM!" he cried.

Fitz grabbed Snitch by the arm and ran as fast as his legs would carry him towards the huge solid doors of the Jewel House. "RUN" Fitz called to Noggin.

Looking over his shoulder Fitz saw the three very angry Ravens heading across the pathway toward them flapping their large wings to run even faster and catching them up with every step.

"Why are they not flying after us?" he called between gasped breaths.

"They can't" gasped Snitch trying desperately to catch his breath as Fitz dragged him along "they have their wings clipped to stop them. Legend says if they leave the tower the kingdom will fall."

"Well, thank you your majesty" whooped Noggin laughing as she ran.

In front of them loomed a big black door with the words "THE CROWN JEWELS" written in gold above but it was shut tight, right behind them catching up every moment were the ravens, they had nowhere to go.

"Run, run, run little intruders" called the Ravens cackling so close behind them Fitz could almost feel their breath on his neck. "We're coming, OFF WITH THEIR HEADS" they crowed as the gap closed behind them and they were snapping at the heels of Fitz and his team.

All of a sudden Fitz saw something move further along the front of the building. A guard had started to move away from his guard box and was marching towards the door, the door that was now starting to open as the change of guard came out.

"Look they're changing the guard" called Fitz whilst pulling an exhausted Snitch along. "Come on hurry up, keep going Snitch we are almost there."

With all their might and using their last bit of energy, they all three ran towards the guard. The Ravens were now so close and with a lunge forward one managed to snap and grab at Fitz's backpack getting a hold for a second.

"LET GO YOU," roared Noggin angrily as she grabbed Fitz's backpack and pulled it free from his beak.

"NOW SLIDE" yelled Fitz and all three dropped to the ground sliding between the marching guard's feet, skidding across the gravel path and stopped behind the huge wheels of one of the cannons that lined the building behind him.

"Pesky Ravens" muttered the guard under his breath as the three black birds giving chase bundled into a squawking pile around his feet.

Behind the row of cannons Fitz, Noggin and Snitch ran and ran with every ounce of energy they had left towards the opening door and the guard marching towards it until finally, they caught up. With a leap, they grabbed his swinging trouser bottoms just as he walked through the Jewel House door.

Noggin stuck out her tongue and blew a loud raspberry at the pile of angry ravens who could only watch as the giant door slammed shut behind them and was locked with a resounding clunk. Once safely inside they quickly dropped from the guard's trousers and ran to hide behind the nearest suit of shining armour. All three collapsed in a heap of exhaustion as they listening to the footsteps echoing around the old building as he marched away

"Boy oh boy, Fat Larry was not kidding, they are evil" wheezed Noggin laying on her back with her eyes screwed up tight trying hard to catch her breath. "I thought they had us there for a moment."

"They didn't look very happy" gasped Snitch holding his sides as his beating heart rang in his ears. "I don't think I have ever been so scared in all my life and I am scared of a lot of things" he declared causing the others to fall about laughing.

"Oh, please don't" cried Noggin "my sides hurt from running" as she winced in pain.

Fitz had caught his breath enough to heave himself up from the floor and, after checking the guard had indeed gone, slowly he walked out from behind the armour and into the middle of the vast room.

He looked around in amazement at the shining suits of armour and the big gold and red woven tapestries and paintings hanging on the walls.

Having recovered from their run in with the ravens Noggin and Snitch appeared at his side. Cupping her hands around her mouth Noggin cried out loudly "Hellloooooo" and then turned her head listening for her own echo

....Hellloooooooooooo....

"*Shush* Noggin" scolded a startled Fitz whilst Snitch giggled naughtily next to him. "Stop playing around, we don't know who can hear us."

"Sorry," said Noggin with a twinkle in here eye winking at Snitch. "So which way?" she asked excitedly looking at all the doors that lead from the room in various directions.

"The guard went that way," said Snitch nodding towards an open door to the side of the room. "Yes, look there it's signed "The Jewel Room" as he pointed to the large sign painted with an arrow.

"Well, what are we waiting for let's go?" insisted Noggin as she ran across the room towards the door, her tiny footsteps echoing off the walls.

"Noggin wait" yelled Fitz after her but as usual she wasn't listening. "Snitch we need some help here, do you have a map of the tower inside?" asked Fitz running after Noggin so as not to lose sight of her.

Clap. The light keyboard appeared and floated in front of Snitch who searched his library, which was not the easiest thing whilst still running after Noggin and watching where he was going.

"Yes, got it" as the map appeared on his glasses with a dot blinking to show where they were. "LEFT THERE" hollered Snitch to Noggin who was now so far out in front of the others they could only just see her.

"Noggin please slow down" shouted Fitz as they ran past more suits of armour and paintings, who's eyes seemed to follow them, all glowing mysteriously in the low yellow lamp light.

"Right Noggin, right through that door and then down the stairs" puffed Snitch. Noggin turned right as instructed and disappeared through the door.

"Stairs have to slow her down *surely*?" cried Fitz as he and Snitch followed through the door and swiftly stopped at the top of a large flight of stone stairs. Following the stairs, attached to the wall was a red rope handrail fastened with large golden hooks that spiralled down and out of sight to the rooms below.

"Where did she go?" asked a confused Snitch.

"I don't know" replied Fitz looking around and down the stairs as far as he could see. "Noggin where are you?"

With that, the red rope handrail on the wall started to wiggle. To their surprise Noggin appeared around the bend in the staircase, balancing on the red rope using it like a tightrope, her arms were outstretched as she walked skilfully one foot in front of the other to balance herself. "Come on slow coaches, this is fun" she beckoned to them as she jumped and turned mid-air like a gymnast on a beam. Putting her arms back out she proceeded to walk out of sight.

"She is truly bonkers" announced Snitch.

"She sure is" laughed Fitz.

Chapter 21

Fluffy Unicorns and Giant Broccoli

Noggin was waiting patiently for them at the bottom. "That was fun" she whooped as the others came to the end of the rope and jumped down to join her. "Look were here" she pointed to a large stone doorway with giant vault doors standing guard either side and, in the centre, a heavy iron grill.

In silence, they stood in the hallway which felt like the safest place in the world to be but also the scariest at the same time. Beyond the door, visible through the barrier was a dimly lit room making it hard to see inside properly. Noggin took a deep breath and started to walk forwards; Fitz quickly grabbed her arm to stop her. "Noggin we have to be careful" he whispered. "We don't know what, or who's in there."

"What do you mean?" questioned Noggin frowning at Fitz. "The ravens are outside, and you saw the pirates boarding 'The Swirling Pearl', you said so yourself."

"Yes, I saw them go onto the ship, but I didn't see the ship actually leave" Fitz corrected her quickly. "We just need to be careful that's all I'm saying."

With caution, they slowly walked towards the mighty doorway and climbed through the holes in the security barrier into the jewel room beyond. All three stopped, eyes wide in amazement at the sight before them.

The room was filled with large glass cases and had a red carpet on the floor, the smell of lavender furniture polish filled the air and it was eerily silent.

Inside each gleaming case lay a blanket of red velvet and upon it rose stands upon which lay large red and gold cushions. Resting on these cushions were the most magnificent jewels and treasures, more breath taking than anything they could have ever imagined.

Each individual case had a spotlight inside that shone down making the jewels within making them shimmer, sparkle and dance. They reflected on the walls and glass cases like magic and shone on the red cushions making the whole room glow as if it were one large jewel itself.

"Oh, my" gasped Noggin in a hushed voice. "That has to be the most beautiful thing I have ever seen."

"Amazing" whispered Snitch and Fitz slowly together as the sparkle of the gems before them glinted in their eyes. As they gazed at the cases before them Fitz became aware of a low rumbling noise coming from either side of them. He turned his head slowly towards the sound coming from his left. There slouched in the corner was a guard sound asleep snoring deeply. It was the same when he glanced right to see a second guard who was also fast asleep snoring quietly and dribbling from the corner of his mouth.

Without warning one of the guards let out a loud yell causing Noggin, Snitch and Fitz to jump backwards in fright and bang into the security barrier.

"STOP IT, STOP IT! I DON'T LIKE FLUFFY UNICORNS" he cried and waved his arm around whilst he twitched as if he were fighting something.

This was followed by the other guard "ARRGGHHH GET OFF, GET OFF GIANT BROCCOLLI SPIDERS... NOOOOO!!!" before they both snorted loudly and continued snoring.

With their hearts beating almost out of their chests in fright the three tiny Dream Drifters froze. "Where did they come from?" gulped Noggin as one guard started to wriggle and twitch, fighting his giant broccoli spider no doubt.

"I think they have been here the whole time" replied Fitz "but I don't think they are supposed to be asleep; I think they are supposed to be guarding the jewels."

"Oh, that's not good" whispered Snitch under his breath as his face started to go pale.

Fitz took a couple of deep breaths to calm himself, what he wouldn't have given for Bysidian to be there right now. "Snitch check the room and check it carefully." Snitch scanned the room thoroughly including the sleeping guards.

"No sign of pirates the coasts clear" he declared.

"Phew," said Noggin. "Come on the crowns are over there," she said as she moved to walk further into the room. Snitch grabbed her arm and pulled her backwards sharply. "I wish you two would stop doing that she" growled pulling her arm out of Snitch's grasp.

"I said no pirates, but there are these," said Snitch as he grabbed a dust bomb from Noggins belt pocket.

"Hey that's mine" she cried as Snitch pulled out the pin and proceeded to roll it across the floor like a bowling ball into the room. There was a loud Poof as the bomb went off and pink dust started to fill the room like a cloud. Gradually it started to settle and through the pink haze, a spider's web of red security lasers covering the entire room began to appear.

"Ah," said Noggin "now they could be a small problem."

"So near, but so far" sighed Snitch looking at the crowns glittering in the case across the far side of the secure room. Fed up he sat down with a bump resting his back against the security grill behind.

Chapter 22

Growing Wings

"We're not giving up now," said a determined Fitz walking a little further into the room as he paced back and forth being careful to stay clear of where the lasers started. "We've come too far, there has to be a way. Noggin any of your gadgets we could use would sure be useful right now."

Noggin moved to his side and started to look around her belt and, in her pockets, thinking hard and checking everything she had. The grappling gun was gone somewhere deep underwater below the bridge as was the light rope left at Big Ben. There were dust bombs, laser light, night vision goggles, sticky gloves, a secret new wand which she really needed to think of a fancy name for, zip line bracelets and a half-eaten bar of gooey melted chocolate.

"Nothing that will get us through *that*," she said waving her clenching her fists at the red lines and stamping her foot in frustration.

"Unless you can grow wings," joked Fitz.

"Err, actually I might be able to help you there" came the reply from Snitch who was grinning like a Cheshire cat. He was looking over his shoulder at something out in the hallway beyond the grill.

Noggin walked over and her face suddenly lit up. "EMBER" she cried "Oh girl are we glad to see you, but how did you find us?"

Ember curved her fiery wings to make her body look like a big ball, puffed up her cheeks and waddled around the hallway at the bottom of the stairs.

"Ah ha, Fat Larry" laughed Fitz.

"Ready for action again?" asked Noggin as Ember looked well rested. The tiny dragon pulled her wings in tight to her body and slid through one of the gaps in the security grill and nudged Noggin fondly. "I'll take that as a yes" she smiled placing a hand gently on Embers neck. "So, what do you think girl, can we can do it?" she asked pointing towards the laser maze before them.

Ember looked at Noggin and then out into the room before she crouched down and nudged Noggin with her tail. Without hesitation Noggin scrambled into the front seat of Embers saddle but when the others tried to follow Ember snorted and stood up causing them to slip off.

"Hey" exclaimed Fitz.

"No wait, Embers right" insisted Noggin. "She needs to be fast and able to move easily, carrying all three of us she'll be weighed down. I'll go I can do it." Fitz and Snitch knew she was right but that did not mean they were not worried about Noggin going alone.

"Be careful and keep your head down," said Snitch.

Fitz knelt down and from his backpack took the purple bag containing the Dream Catcher Pearl. "You'll need this," he said handing it to Noggin who tied it tightly to her belt. "We'll keep watch here but we cannot get to you to help if anything happens" he reminded her with worry in his voice.

Noggin nodded. "I know Fitz don't worry" she reassured him. "Ok girl, over to you, we need to be at that case over there so do your thing."

Ember lifted off the floor, her head held high so she could see clearly with her feet and tail down towards the ground as if she was standing in the air. She hovered for a moment with her wings flapping strongly forwards and backwards in a figure of eight looking for the best way to get her precious cargo to the case. With a drop of her head, she raised her tail and flew towards the lasers.

Fitz and Snitch watched in awe as Ember darted across the room between the glowing lasers like a red bullet. She skilfully twisted and turned, pulling her wings in tight against her body for small spaces, then spreading them wide like a sail when she needed to slow down for a tricky gap.

Noggin held on tight and closed her eyes, lying forward almost flat in her seat with her legs tucked in tightly to the little dragon's side whose warmth and every breath she could feel beneath her. She did not want to slow Ember down or catch a beam and set the alarm off.

On reaching the case Ember threw open her wings wide, and having stopped completely in the air, dropped slowly to the ground avoiding any last beams of light and landing on the stone floor below. Noggin opened her eyes and looked back at her teammates.

"GO EMBER" they called jumping around and hugging each other.

Noggin patted Ember "glad to have you back" she whispered in her ear and slid out of the warm saddle making sure to staying close to her scaly side.

Towering above them was the crown's case with the jewels inside reflecting in the glass. Noggin reached deep into her pockets and pulled out the two sticky gloves that were black and as the name implies very, very sticky.

Slipping them on she placed one hand on the bottom of the case in front of her, then the next a little higher, then higher and higher using her feet to balance. She started to climb like a spider up a wall until she was finally level with the jewels inside.

"What can you see?" called Fitz feeling a little impatient and frustrated he couldn't see for himself. "Snitch can you see?" he asked but Snitch shook his head.

"My glasses don't work very well with the lasers they are just too bright it makes everything blurry."

Noggin called back. "I can see the crowns and there are swords and a golden ball, an eagle and other things in here." One of the sleeping guards grumbled and turned on his side a little before putting in his thumb and going back to sleep.

"Do you see anything that looks like a Nightmare Pearl?" called Snitch keeping one watchful eye on the guard in case he woke.

"Snitch there are lots and lots of pearls in here" called back Noggin. "Shush a moment and let me look." She looked at the crowns one by one, but it was really hard to see clearly with the reflections of everything else outside on the glass. "I'm going to have to go inside" she called back to the others.

Chapter 23

Very Sparkly

Balancing herself with her toes and her one gloved hand Noggin removed her other glove with her teeth. This seemed like a good idea at the time until it became stuck on her lips and then her front teeth, leaving it hanging from her mouth.

"Is everything all right?" called Snitch.

"Gine efrytings gine" called back Noggin turning her head so the others could not see as she started to panic, and her cheeks shone red with embarrassment. Looking down for help Noggin stared at Ember, but Ember just shrugged and grinned a little. She couldn't move easily for fear of setting the alarms off and besides, Ember decided it was so much funnier to leave the glove where it was. "Ganks fur noting" mumbled back Noggin through sticky teeth.

Maybe, if she got it wet it might not be so sticky and it would simply drop off her lips, well the only way to do that was to lick it of course. Noggin wiggled her tongue inside her gummy lips and across her teeth trying to wet the glove but all that did was proceed to get her tongue stuck as well. Rolling her eyes in her head at her own stupidity she thought to herself, if Snitch ever saw this, he would never let her forget it, ever.

There was only one thing to do. Noggin pressed her mouth hard to the glass, sticking the glove outside her mouth to the shiny surface, she shut her eyes and pulled back hard.

"OOOOOOOWWWW" cried

Noggin as her lips stretched like an elastic band. It pulled her tongue until it stuck out and her teeth felt like they were being pulled out before there was a

snap and a twang as the glove pulled away from her
face like a piece of elastic and stuck fast to the glass
case.

"What was that she said?" asked Fitz.

"I'm not sure" replied Snitch "Its sounded like
she was singing but really, really badly. Noggin
stop messing around and focus we don't have time
for singing" he called crossly.

Leaving the offending glove stuck fast to the
case and with her lips and tongue tingling like they
were on fire Noggin reached into her pockets and
removed her new secret wand (still to be named).

Using the tip Noggin proceeded to slowly draw a
circle around the wet sticky glove that was just big
enough for her body to fit through. Once the two
ends of the circle connected there was a small plink
and the glass and glove within disappeared like
magic.

"Well, that's impressive. Another new toy?"
called Snitch.

Noggin nodded and tried to smile through her sore lips extremely pleased it had worked and also relieved that they had obviously not seen her little issue with the stuck glove. She worked so hard with the Guardians in their workshop on new gadgets but however much they tried them the real test was always out on the missions when they were truly needed.

Carefully Noggin climbed inside the glass case, on her hand the remaining sticky glove. How was she going to get it off? She thought for a moment and then with a sigh and a roll of her eyes she slapped her hand on the glass case and pulled down slipping her hand effortlessly out of the glove.

"Honestly Noggin now why didn't I do that before?" she muttered to herself feeling silly. Small puffs of smoke rose past her from the floor below as Ember chuckled to herself.

Inside the case, the air was still and dusty, it was so quiet she could hear her heart beating. Removing her last dust bomb Noggin cracked the top open ever so slightly.

"Better to be safe than sorry," she thought to herself lifting the top ever so slightly and releasing a tiny squirt of pink dust into the case

hissssssssssssssssss.

To her delight, no lasers appeared. Noggin threw the closed bomb into the case and quickly stuck her fingers in her ears as it hit the velvet covered floor with a thud. Phew, no pressure pad alarms either it was all clear. Through the clearing pink dust, three crowns began to appear. All were different and all glistening with countless magnificent jewels the likes of which Noggin could have never imagined, including hundreds of pearls.

"Which one? Which one?" she said softly looking at each in turn. As Noggin stood looking

Fitz suddenly remembered something the pirates mentioned.

"They said the crown had been taken from the case."

"Who did?" questioned Snitch.

"The pirates, the pirates said the crown had been taken from the case whilst Solomon Fear was still inside, it must have been needed for something by the Queen. Snitch what has the Queen been doing in the last couple of days?"

Snitch's fingers worked like lightning on his keyboard, "Of course," he said loudly. "NOGGIN YOU WANT THE IMPERIAL STATE CROWN" he shouted. "The Queen opened parliament with it on only yesterday."

Noggin had been concentrating so hard on the crowns she jumped at the sound of Snitch's yelling. Turning back towards the hole in the glass she wailed back "WILL YOU STOP YELLING AT ME" and instantly burst into floods of tears.

"Oh boy," said Fitz "It's in there, look at her just like in the vault at home" he whispered to Snitch. "NOGGIN, NOGGIN IT'S THE PEARL" he shouted. "FIGHT IT NOGGIN, FIGHT IT."

By now Noggin had huge fat salty tears rolling down her freckled cheeks, she closed her eyes tightly and took deep breaths, but they just wouldn't stop.

"Lean out of the case" called Snitch.

Noggin placed her hands either side of the hole which was now just a blur through her tear filled eyes and leant forward a little as she tried with all her might to stop crying.

A warm breeze wafted up from below that ruffled her hair and eyelashes softly making her close her eyes and instantly she felt her tears magically dry up. Noggin looked down at Ember who was now head held high breathing up the glass case. She smiled at her faithful friend below.

"Thanks girl. Ok, Snitch what does the crown look like as there are a few in here?"

"Oh well, it's sparkly, very sparkly" he called back unable to resist winding Noggin up as he cheekily winked at Fitz.

"Snitch when I get out of this case you had better run fast, I warn you" Noggin replied calmly looking out of the hole in the case. "AS I AM GOING TO BOP YOU ON THE NOSE SO HARD" she snapped tears starting to flow down her face again.

Snitch chuckled. "Well, it *is* sparkly" he continued "with a big diamond on the band. Above that is a huge deep red ruby on a diamond covered square, it's lined in purple velvet and on top is a diamond covered ball topped with a square that has a blue sapphire in its centre."

Noggin turned and looked at each crown in turn. "Red ruby, diamond ball, got it" she called back and started to move across the case rubbing her flowing tears away on her arm. Carefully she clambered past all the other crowns and jewelled objects up and up and up until she reached the Imperial State Crown.

It was indeed very sparkly Snitch was right. Noggin could see hundreds of different reflections of her own tiny face in all the different sized diamonds and jewels before her. Slowly she started to walk around the crown examining every single pearl she could see until finally, she arrived back at the front where she started.

"It's not here" she sobbed in despair as the tears got faster and faster.

"*UP*" shouted Fitz and Snitch "you have to go *up*, there are pearls further up at the top". Noggin turned towards them nodding but she couldn't see them at all through her pouring tears.

Reaching up Noggin slipped her hand around a small diamond and tried to pull herself up, but her hands were so wet from wiping her face she slipped back down in a crumpled heap on the cushion below. With that, she burst into more uncontrollable sobbing.

Seeing Noggin in such despair Fitz and Snitch were now desperately calling from across the room for her get out of the case and come back. "NO," thought Noggin to herself she was not going to quit and most of all she was not a cry baby, enough was enough. Getting to her feet again with more determination than ever she stood before the crown.

"Oh no, please tell me she's not going to" cried Snitch. With that Noggin buried her face deep into the white fur band around the crown, wiping her eyes and hands dry and then promptly blew her nose very hard. "OHHHH NO" yelled Snitch as Fitz threw his hands over his eyes in disbelief. "Dream Drifter bogies on the Queen's crown *YUCK!*"

Fitz was now peeping out through his fingers. "Better?" he called to Noggin who turned and grinned waving both hands which were now very dry.

Snitch was now on the floor crying tears of laughter at his friend. "Such a lady."

Again, Noggin reached up and got a tight grip on the diamonds in their golden frame above, pulling herself up using the small jewels and their gold mountings like a climbing frame. She went up past the giant glowing red ruby which proved a little slippery, then clambered onto a band of diamonds that stretched directly up to the very top of the crown. With her tears starting to flow again Noggin climbed quickly checking every pearl as she passed them. Finally, she arrived at the top and there before her was the diamond encrusted globe, but what was happening?

Now as well as crying she started to feel the panic rising inside her, she felt scared as the hairs on her neck stood up and she could feel the anger rising from her toes like a fire running up her legs. After looking down at her boots for a second

Noggin suddenly realised exactly what was happening.

Slowly getting to her knees Noggin leaned out over the edge looking underneath.   There hanging below her were four big drop pearls dangling like raindrops above the purple velvet fabric of the crown. Three were golden and dazzling but the one directly below her wasn't. The pearl below her was black and swirling, in its side a small crack causing a tiny stream of mist to escape from its shell which hung around it like a shadowy fog.

"Found you" she whispered.

Chapter 24

Dragon Pearls

Getting back to her feet Noggin turned towards the blurry images of her teammates standing in the distance across the room.

"IT'S HERE" she yelled back, the sound echoing around the case. Huge tears were now running like a river from her chin in big drips. "I found it it's here, hanging underneath" she called waving her arms frantically at her friends across the room.

Fitz and Snitch could just see Noggin waving at them. Her voice was heavy in tears and her throat sore from shouting at them in anger, so they could not hear her properly.

"What is she saying?" asked Snitch. "I can't hear her but she's waving and shouting about something." Fitz waved back and then placed a hand behind each ear to signal Noggin they could not hear. Noggins anger rose and rose, crosser and crosser causing the pearl below her to grow even blacker beneath her tiny feet.

With tears flowing and anger rising Noggin dropped and slid down the diamond crown. Bouncing across the ruby she landed back on the cushion below. Then stumbling back to her feet, she ran for the gap in the case and the clean nightmare free air beyond.

"I SAID IT'S HERE, I FOUND IT"

she screamed at the top of her lungs as she poked her head out of the hole in the case causing her huge tears to gather on the glass outside and slide slowly down.

"*Yes*, I knew you could do it" called back Fitz giving a huge sigh of relief. He and Snitch were both just a little shocked at just actually how loud Noggin could shout.

"What do I need to do now, it's got a crack in it and its leaking nightmare?" called Noggin.

"Use the Dream Catcher Pearl I gave you, snap it open and trap the Nightmare Pearl inside it's the only way to stop it." Noggin nodded and with a few deep breaths of the clear air outside turned ready to return to the crown when there came a gasp from Snitch.

"NOGGIN WAIT" he shouted before turning to Fitz. "If the pearl is taken there will be a gap in the crown where it used to be, we *can't* leave it like that the humans will know someone was here."

Noggin grabbed the purple bag from her belt and rummaged around pulling out the white Dream Catcher Pearl inside. "Only one in here and I need that to capture the Nightmare Pearl." As she held the pearl out, she felt a warm waft of wind again from below and looked down towards Ember who was still waiting patiently below.

"What is it girl?" asked Noggin curiously as Ember looked up the glass case as if trying to tell her something.

Sliding down the glass like crystal droplets were Noggins big fat tears and as they all met, they were making one large droplet of salty water. That droplet was trickling down towards Ember who had stretched her head up on her long elegant neck and was now blowing warm air up the case side.

"Whoa girl, careful that's getting very hot" called Noggin pulling her face back inside the case out of the stream of hot air. The instance Noggin was safe inside Ember took a deep breath, filling her mighty lungs. Then she blew with all her strength aiming at the large droplet of tears sliding towards her, a stream of vivid blue flames and white smoke shot from Embers mouth.

In amazement Fitz, Snitch and, from inside the case, Noggin watched as the water droplet started to glow. It glowed like liquid glass swirling with every colour of the rainbow and mixed with it was a haze of white from Embers smoke. As fast as the flames had started, they stopped and as it dropped Ember caught in her mouth a bead of glass that shimmered and shined perfectly just like a pearl.

Noggin popped her head out of the case and looked down at her friend below.

"Did you know she could do that?" called Fitz almost speechless from amazement.

"No, I didn't" called back Noggin grinning widely at Ember below. "You never stop amazing me," she said quietly to her fiery friend.

The Dragon Pearl still carefully held in her mouth Ember waited patiently as Noggin lowered the purple bag on its golden thread. When it was close enough Ember dropped the new Dragon Pearl inside. With the bag now containing the two pearls safely on her belt, the tears and anger gone, Noggin started to again climb the crown. On reaching the top she opened the bag removing the Dream Catcher Pearl.

Holding firmly to both sides of the pearl she twisted them in opposite directions, opening the tiny pearl case with a blast of icy wind. The cold wind blew inside the case like a whirlwind whistling around and around almost knocking Noggin over. It took all her strength to lower herself to her knees before slowly leaning out to face the Nightmare Pearl below. The anger inside Noggin was now so strong every muscle in her body felt tight and shaky whilst rivers of tears streamed down her face. Her hair whipped around stinging her face and the four pearls dangling below the crown lashed around trying to break free in the gale.

With a deep breath to calm her shaking hands, she reached out focusing on the black Nightmare Pearl swinging around before her and as it swung between the two halves of the Dream Catcher Pearl, she slammed them shut.

Noggin pulled the Dream Catcher Pearl up to her face and watched captivated by the black fog swirling inside as it got blacker and blacker as the imprisoned Nightmare Pearl tried to release its sadness and pain.

"NOGGIN, NOGGIN HAVE YOU GOT IT? ARE YOU ALRIGHT?" came the anxious cry from across the room.

Noggin turned towards the voices and as she did one last large tear flew off her cheek landing with a splash on her hand. All of a sudden, the trapped Nightmare Pearl slipped from her grasp and bounced down the crown, landing on the red velvet case floor below.

"Mm well I *did* have it" she called back to the others, "but I dropped it."

"YOU DID WHAT?" squealed Snitch in a high voice whilst trying to look through his glasses before pulling them off quickly as he was blinded by the lasers.

"Can you see it, is it still in one piece?" called Fitz giving Snitch a shove with his elbow to be quiet so he could hear.

"Yes, I can see it it's just below me near the long golden stick thing" Noggin replied waving her hand in its general direction "and yes, it's still in one piece." Fitz held his head in relief as Snitch sat down with a wobbly thump as his legs gave way. He was feeling very faint again.

Reaching inside the bag Noggin carefully hung the replacement Dragon Pearl in the now empty tiny clasp on the crown, giving it a little nudge so it swung and sparkled just like the other three.

"Perfect" she smiled.

Chapter 25

Run

Using the crown like a giant slide Noggin slid down and jumped onto a long golden pole laying across the case. Running along it, she jumped down at the end, scooping up the dropped Dream Catcher Pearl as she landed elegantly like a gymnast on a beam. With the pearl tightly tucked under her arm so as not to drop it again, Noggin turned and stumbled backwards in surprise.

Before her was the biggest diamond she had ever seen and shining back to her from it were lots of wibbly wobbly reflections of her own face. "The star of Africa" she read on a plaque by its side and started to giggle as she pulled faces and the reflections did the same back, moving closer and further away to make them bigger or smaller.

"You have to see this, it's got a real star in this one" she called back to the others giggling. "It's so funny" as she crossed her eyes and stuck out her tongue.

"Please, Noggin can we just go home now" pleaded Snitch getting anxious. "Stop messing around" but Noggin didn't answer, and she had stopped pulling faces. She was now frozen staring at the huge diamond with terror on her white face. Staring back at her was not just her own reflection.

From the other side of the mighty diamond, another face was grinning at her through the jewel. A craggy, rugged face furrowed with wrinkles and scars. One eye was staring black and evil like the ravens outside and the other was covered with a large leather patch. Both were sunken into dark shadows by thick black eyebrows. With hair as black as the night that was swept back with a piece of tattered snakeskin and through the unruly beard gleamed one golden tooth.

Noggin pulled the pearl to her chest grasping it so tightly her knuckles went white and took a few steps backwards very slowly. Without a blink or breath, she did not take her eyes off the face beyond the diamond.

"Come on Noggin" called Fitz "lets' get out of here it's not safe what's wrong with you?"

"Run" she tried to shout but all that came out was a faint squeak. There was a flash of black and suddenly the face was gone giving Noggin her chance. "RUN, SNITCH, FITZ, RUN!" she screamed at the top of her voice as she turned and ran with all her might to get to the hole in the case.

As if from thin air Solomon Fear appeared standing on the golden pole attached to the huge diamond, his long black ragged coat swung around his tattered leather boots with the scruffy collar turned up. By his side hung a long sword and, in his hand, he held a long thin black cane, topped with a silver serpents head matching the figurehead on his ship outside. Noggin leapt as she finally reached the hole to warn the others but looking out her eyes were met with a sight that made her gasp out loud in shock.

"NO, NO, NO" she shrieked across the room as she saw Fitz and Snitch struggling and fighting with all their might to get free from the Pirates that were now seizing them tightly and laughing loudly.

"Tut, tut, tut little lady…I believe that belongs to me" Solomon said calmly in a low deep voice as he lifted his cane and pointed at the pearl firmly in Noggins grasp. "It's not nice to steal you know" he smirked waggling the end of his cane as the other pirates beyond the lasers cackled at their captain.

"Aye, it's not nice to steal lady didn't you know that?" one bawled back loudly, trying to ignore

Snitch who was stamping on his foot as hard as he could and kicking him in the leg. *"Ouch,* you little worm" the pirate snapped at Snitch. "Will you stay still and stop wriggling" as he tightened his grip.

"What do you want us to do with these two Captain?" called the other who now had Fitz down face first on the floor sat on him as it was the only way to get him to stay still. Fitz looked across at the guards still snoring either side of him willing one of them to just wake up.

"Ah now see that's not going to work," the pirate said following Fitz's stare. "They are fast out and will be for a few more hours yet thanks to the Captains sleep dust. We couldn't have them in the way you see. They will wake up with a sore head but none the wiser we were ever here" he smirked.

Solomon Fear jumped down and slowly walked across the red velvet floor towards Noggin who was sat now shaking in fear with her back firmly against the glass case side beside the hole. She had her arm entwined around the pearl gripping it with all her might and could hear Ember moving below.

"Take them to the Swirling Pearl" he ordered with his gaze still firmly on Noggin, "but do it quietly in case there are more guards around" he hissed.

"Ooh do it quietly" whispered one pirate to the other in a silly voice as he stood up, trying to hold the struggling Fitz. "Did you hear that? As if that's an easy thing to do with these two,

oooouucchhh!" as Fitz kicked him in the shin hard.

Noggin glanced out of the corner of her eye down to Ember below. Should she drop her the pearl? If she did then Solomon Fear would be upon Noggin in a flash. If she jumped, she wouldn't be able to catch onto Ember with her hands full and would crash to the floor cracking open the pearl and triggering the alarms. The purple bag was tied to her belt, but she was sat on it and she couldn't reach it easily without taking her eyes off Solomon Fear.

The evil pirate captain had walked calmly and slowly across the case and was now so close to Noggin her nose stung with the smell of all the nightmares, fear and pain that ran through his evil body. "Now hand me the pearl and we can all go home" he demanded through his yellow teeth stretching out his hand and grabbing for Noggins precious cargo.

"NO, LEAVE HER ALONE, NOGGIN GIVE IT TO HIM" cried Fitz who had managed to bite the struggling pirate's hand across his mouth.

"I SAID GET THEM OUT OF HERE" yelled Solomon crossly at his crew.

"Let's go" shouted the sore handed pirate dragging Fitz. "I've just about had enough of you goodie, goodie Dream Drifters."

Chapter 26

Smokey Darkness

"Well, that's not very nice is it?" came the familiar voice above their heads followed by a large winged shadow and rush of air. Suddenly Fitz and Snitch were standing free and the pirates holding them had completely disappeared.

Before them soaring gracefully through the lasers rode Bysidian Black on his sleek silver dragon Argent, the two mean pirates were dangling from his claws wriggling and squirming trying to get free.

"Thought you may need a little help" he called back as Argent skilfully dodged the red lines flying towards to the suits of armour at the side of the room. Each pirate was dropped in turn so their scruffy coat collars caught on the sharp pikes each soldier held and they were left dangling in mid-air helplessly.

"NOGGINS IN THE CASE, BYSIDIAN HELP HER" yelled Snitch at the top of his lungs pointing.

"Well, well Solomon long time no see" declared Bysidian arriving by the case.

"THROW AND JUMP" he yelled to Noggin who did exactly as she was told and launched the pearl to Argent who caught it in his powerful claws as she threw herself through the hole just as Solomon Fear pounced. His long filthy black fingernails scraped along Noggins belt as she fell through the gap and dropped into thin air.

"NO!" screamed Solomon Fear "I NEED YOU TO GET ME OUT OF HERE" he cried after her in rage.

With a rush, faithful Ember flew up the case towards the falling Noggin who just managed to grab the saddle with one arm as they met. Noggin threw herself into the seat and held on tight.

Throwing back his sleek head Argent roared as a mighty blast of white of hot flames poured from his mouth melting the glass hole shut leaving a screaming Solomon Fear trapped inside.

"That will teach him" laughed Bysidian as the fearsome pirate captain banged on the glass with his clenched fists and a face red with anger. "He'll have a long wait until they open that case again and he can escape undetected."

Noggin clung to Ember with all her remaining strength as they followed Argent back through the room until they reached Fitz and Snitch who were waiting by the door. Noggin dropped from the saddle and landed on her wobbly legs exhausted as they threw their arms around her in relief, she was safe.

"Time for this later" hurried Bysidian. "We're not clear yet, here take the pearl and tie it safe inside your bag then let's go home."

Noggin handed Fitz the bag and taking the pearl from Argents grasp placed the precious pearl inside before climbing aboard Ember followed by the others.

"You do know I *hate* this bit?" huffed Snitch. Both dragons turned and looked at him. Snitch smiled "but after everything that's happened today, there is nowhere I would rather be."

"I think you have a new friend" whispered Noggin to Ember as she smiled a little, if dragons do smile that is.

"HEY, YOU CAN'T JUST LEAVE US HERE" came the cry across the room from one of the dangling pirates who were swinging like Christmas baubles on a tree.

"No, get us down" cried the other before they ...." with that there was a groan and a mumble from the sleeping guards.

"THEY'RE WAKING UP, GET US OUT OF HERE" came the cries as they wriggled so much their coats ripped, dropping them into the lasers below. The noise was deafening as the alarms burst into action, lights flashed, and the solid steel vault doors started to close.

"GO,GO,GO," hollered Bysidian as Argent soared into the air followed immediately by Ember. Holding so tight he thought his fingers may snap Snitch glanced back to see Solomon Fear screaming in rage as he swung his sword with both hands at the glass case. The glass shattered into millions of pieces like an explosion and the once trapped Solomon Fear leapt into thin air.

With an almighty swoop of their huge wings, the two dragons shot towards the closing doors and with the gap between them almost closed they turned on their sides and shot through like bullets from a gun. The steel doors clamped shut behind them clang protecting the Jewel room and all its treasures safely inside.

Like a pair of silver and red rockets, the two dragons flew up the stairs and out along the huge corridors. First, they flew high, then low swerving and darting, to avoid the guards who were now running towards the Jewel room. Shutter doors were slamming shut all around them the sound echoing along the corridors, they were getting trapped inside the building.

Flying against the stream of guards Argent zipped inside a door labelled 'Guard Room' and stopped. The room was now empty with steaming cups of coffee and food left abandoned on the tables in the commotion, there was a small kitchen area with some tattered comfy chairs and "A FIREPLACE" yelled Fitz.

"And that means a chimney" finished Bysidian the two dragons threw back their wings and launched themselves into the smoky darkness beyond. As they went up and up the soot made it hard to breathe making the tiny Dream Drifters cough and it stung their eyes. Both dragons had no such problems they were born from fire and it felt like home.

All of a sudden and with great relief, they shot out of the top of the chimney with a *pop* like corks from a champagne bottle, into the cool, soot free starry night air. Like a parachute, both dragons whipped open their wings stopping in mid-air for a moment before dropping to land on the cannon lined pathway below.

Coughing and spluttering the trio slid off Embers back, rubbing their blackened eyes whilst Bysidian shook his cloak and dusted off his armour.

"Look," coughed Fitz pointing beyond Bysidian to the sky above.

There rising above the fortress walls and into the cold night sky was 'The Swirling Pearl'. Its sails were full of air and pirates hung from the masts securing the ropes. The dark silhouette of Solomon

Fear stood at the back turning the ships wheel and bellowing orders to his crew as they sailed into the night sky, its skull and crossbones waving as they sailed out of view with its stolen Queens pearl treasure.

"Well, well, well look who it is lads, they just can't keep away and see they've brought a friend" came the voice. A huge raven walked out of the darkness behind one cannon towards them.

Quickly Bysidian turned from where the ship had gone from view and reached for his sword. Like a flash, he moved to stand with the two dragons defiantly between the team and the glossy black bird.

"Yes, they can't keep away boss" came another voice as a second Raven appeared from below the next cannon, followed by a third, then a fourth. "Sounds like you've been causing some trouble," said Cedric. "Just listen to all that commotion and the alarms and all the blue lights and sirens coming across the bridge, what have you been doing?"

"Thieving I bet," said another Raven. "A band of little thieves" he sniggered, "and we don't like thieves do we boss?" The Ravens got closer and closer to their tiny prey their beady black eyes sparkling and sharp beaks threatening.

"No Odin we certainly do not like thieves, you know what we do with thieves don't you?"

"Oh, we do we do" came the chorus from the Ravens gathering around their boss.

"OFF WITH THEIR HEADS" Cedric called with a flap of his wings as the Ravens lunged at the dragons, Bysidian and the three frightened Dream Drifters.

Chapter 27

A Bit of Magic

"GERONIMO" came the cry as a large ball of grey feathers and pink knobbly legs appeared from nowhere, sending the startled Ravens flying in every direction like skittles in a bowling alley.

"CAN'T STOP, NO BRAKES" he hollered just in time for everyone else to jump out of the way as Fat Larry bundled past them in a ball, crashing into the nearest cannon wheel, landing with a thump, legs, wings and feathers everywhere. Noggin gasped.

"Larry" she cried rushing over to the dazed pigeon followed by Fitz and Snitch leaving Bysidian and the dragons looking puzzled at the bundle of feathers and legs on the floor, wondering exactly what or who it was.

Back on his feet, Fat Larry shook his head. "Oh, that hurt," he said as Noggin went to hug him.

"What are you doing here I thought you never came in, I thought you flew home?"

"Oh no not now little friend," said Larry. "We've got to go," he said hastily pointing towards the Ravens who were now back on their feet, running back towards them now very, very cross indeed.

"HE'S RIGHT, LET'S GO" yelled Bysidian from Argents back as Fitz and Snitch jumped aboard Ember and held on. The two dragons and Fat Larry, carrying Noggin, launched from the ground just as the band of ravens reached them, snapping at Fat Larry's tail.

"*OOOWWW!! HEY!*" squealed Fat Larry looking down as they left the huddle of mean shouting Ravens below. "That's my feather you've got there" as Cedric spat it out of his beak angrily in disgust.

Once safely outside the walls of the Tower, away from all the commotion inside, the two tiny dragons and Fat Larry landed by the river.

"Larry you're a hero *again*" cried Noggin hugging him the best she could around his neck. He was so big, and she was so tiny.

"That certainly was brave," said Bysidian Black walking over to Larry. "Thank you."

"And this isn't the first time he's saved us either" explained Snitch who retold the rescue on Tower Bridge.

"Ah stop" cooed Larry "you're embarrassing me" he smiled with a waft of his wing.

"What made you come back, we saw you fly away home and I thought you never went inside the Tower walls?" asked Noggin curiously, sliding off his round smooth feathered back.

"Well, now I was flying home, that was the plan anyway" started Fat Larry, "but I decided to stop and have a little snooze on the way just down there," he said pointing with his wing at a large tree a little way down the riverbank.

Fitz smiled along with the others. "*WOW* you did get a long way" he joked. Larry glanced at him for being cheeky which made them all giggle and continued.

"That's where I met her, my Petunia" he sighed and cooed lovingly. "She is the most beautiful pigeon I've ever seen" he drifted off starry eyed. "So, I decided to stay around here for a while maybe try a new home and a change of scenery, away from that noisy palace. Anyway, there I was just snoozing in the tree when Petunia woke me up saying she had just seen the most beautiful shooting star come from the sky and fly inside the Tower, which I now know of course was Bysidian on Argent. All of a sudden there were alarms and lights and shouting, Petunia was scared but I knew it had to be you in trouble? I couldn't just leave you I'm part of the team after all" he said proudly fluffing out his chest in pride.

"You certainly are" smiled back Fitz nodding.

From the tree, a pigeon started to call softly, and Fat Larry turned. "Time to go," he said curling his wings around Noggin, Fitz and Snitch and squeezing so hard they were buried in his feathers. "Safe journey home teammates" he called back as he flew towards Petunias call. "Remember if you ever need me you know where to find me."

They all watched as Fat Larry, missing a tail feather, disappeared along the river bank and into the large tree in the distance. Back to his new home with his love Petunia where he belonged.

With Fat Larry gone Noggin turned to Bysidian. "So, what I would like to know is how did you find us and how did you know we might need just a little help?" she questioned.

"Yes, I was wondering that as well" added a curious Snitch.

Bysidian smiled and climbed out of his saddle. "With a bit of magic," he said gently rubbing his hand across Argent's side. The silver scales started to shimmer and ripple like the clearest water on a sunny day and then an image appeared that slowly got clearer and clearer.

"Hey that's all of us" exclaimed Snitch waving his hand slowly around. "Well, it's the back of us anyway," he said puzzled. Fitz turned around, " well now I can see your face but not ours," said Snitch even more confused. Bysidian laughed as all three turned and looked at the only thing stood behind them, Ember. As she blinked the image flickered. "Well, I'll be," said Snitch "you spy on us with the dragons, you see what they see."

"Yes, yes we do" replied Bysidian as he rubbed his hands across Argents side and the scales returned to normal again. "Do you *really* think the

208

Guardians and I would send you out to face the nightmares you do without keeping an eye on you? We did, however, lose you at the palace for a while, all we could see was a lot of brown hair then snuffling and darkness and a lot of snoring, which did concern us a little" he grinned knowingly at Ember.

The night sky was now lighting up with the morning dawn so Bysidian slipped back into Argent's saddle. "Time to go home" he announced. Fitz stopped and removing the purple bag containing the trapped Nightmare Pearl he carefully handed it over.

"Take this," he said quietly. "Take it home to the vault where it's safe and free your team, we have one more thing to do and we will be right behind you," he said looking at the other two.

"Now that reminds me," said Bysidian in a whisper to Fitz reaching under his cloak. "The High Minister sent you this."

As Argent and Bysidian disappeared from view, leaving a thin silver trail in the sky as the only evidence they were ever there, Fitz took his seat on Embers saddle.

"So, girl, do you think you could find your way back?"

As the birds started to sing the dawn chorus welcoming the new day, the tiny dew dancers skipped and whizzed across the lawn, dropping their morning dew on the blades of grass and spiderwebs. Ember gracefully landed on the sill outside the still open window. Inside the Queen was in bed asleep tossing and turning, no doubt having a really bad dream again caused by the leaking Nightmare Pearl she had worn in her crown.

With Noggin and Snitch tucked safely out of view behind the curtains Ember glided across the room, watched only by the corgi next to the low burning fire who had shared his bed with her. Carefully she dropped onto the bedcovers just below the large pillow the queen was resting on. Fitz slid from the tiny dragon's saddle and took off his backpack watching the Queen just in case she woke from her terrible nightmare.

Reaching right inside to the bottom of his bag Fitz pulled out a white velvet bag tied with a white and gold rope and opened it lifting out the most beautiful glowing tiny golden pearl the others had ever seen.

"Now where on earth did that come from?" whispered Snitch.

"The white bags only come from the High Minister himself" gasped Noggin.

"A special Dream Pearl for a special lady" smiled Snitch as Fitz crawled just under the sleeping Queens pillow, leaving the glorious tiny pearl to do it magic.

As Ember flew from the bed and landed to collect Noggin and Snitch the sky outside started to glow a magnificent orange as the sun rose. Fitz turned to see the Queen peacefully sleeping a smile upon her face.

Their work was done.

Chapter 28

Escape

Fitz and his team dropped into Dreamcast mountain just as night fell over the island, landing next to a snoring Argent but with no sign of Bysidian. Leaving Ember with Argent to rest Fitz, Noggin and Snitch slid down the tunnel slide and ran towards the mighty Granite Vault as fast as their tired legs would carry them.

Turning the corner, they saw Bysidian grasping the trapped Nightmare Pearl in his hand running through the repaired vault door. It was still leaking a thick black fog inside its Dream Catcher Pearl prison as the once white pearl turned blacker and blacker and starting to moan.

"I have to hurry" called Bysidian as they all ran across the vault towards the shadows and the Nightmare Vault door. "WAIT HERE, NOT YOU" as he ran through the cold vault door. He gave it a hard push behind him thinking it had closed, but his push was not quite hard enough and the door stopped open a crack just enough for a curious Fitz to push it gently open a little.

The walls of swirling Nightmare Pearls around him were blacker than before as another was brought into the vault, the whistling wind got stronger and colder and the moaning grew louder.

In the centre of the room, Bysidian took a purple crystal from his armour throwing it in the air as he had before, casting a purple glow across the room. As they watched silently the leader of The Night Warriors stopped. Taking his sword, he placed the blade tip first into one of the dragon's eye holes in the stone floor and with a sharp turn, there was a loud clunk like an old lock being undone with a key. Bysidian stepped back as part of the vault floor opened and out of it rose a large black column topped with an open silver dragon's claw. Raising the black Dream Catcher Pearl high above his head and with all his might he threw it to the floor, smashing its shell and releasing the Nightmare Pearl within.

Stumbling backwards in shock for a moment the three then watched as he placed the leaking Nightmare Pearl inside the grasp of the silver dragon's claw where the talons clanked shut holding it fast. The black fog was growing and growing from the pearl stronger and stronger. Without warning a blinding bright flash of light shone out from the crack which got brighter and brighter as the crack started to grow and grow. The Nightmare Pearl was splitting in half.

From beyond the bright light, a sword appeared tip first, followed by a hand grasping the handle then and arm covered in the same armour Bysidian wore. The armour was dented and scratched from battle as one of his Night Warriors started to escape from the pearl.

As one climbed out and dropped to the vault floor exhausted Bysidian helped him to his feet. Another and another followed until four, battle weary Night Warriors were stood in the vault. With the last Warrior free the light from the pearl grew brighter and brighter until it was almost blinding.

Suddenly from the pearl came a loud wail and a deafening howl. Bysidian looked across the vault horror on his face when he spotted the open door and the three terrified faces peeping in. He ran across the vault towards them just as the blinding bright light filled the room behind him. Grabbing the mighty vault door, he slammed it shut with them safely on the other side.

First, the ground started to rumble below their feet shaking and shaking until they almost lost their balance, then the door started to bulge making the wailing face on it move as if opening its mouth wider and wider. All three ran only stopping when safely in the middle of the golden lit Granite Vault.

Silence...

The wailing stopped, the floor was still and, after what seemed like an eternity, the vault door clanked and then groaned open. The vault beyond was again in darkness as Bysidian walked out followed by his rescued team. The weary Night Warriors pulled the door tightly closed making sure it was locked shut behind them. They walked over to the three tiny Dream Drifters who stood silently in shock from the sight they had just witnessed and also the sight of five Night Warriors stood in front of them. Until this morning they did not even know they were real.

Bysidian introduced his team Fabian Feldspar, Templar Storm, Lucius Squall and Quillion Quartz.

217

"We believe we have you to thank for saving us?" said Fabian Feldspar shaking Fitz's hand.

"Bysidian's told us what you did and that was beyond brave," said Templar Storm the others nodding in agreement. "If you ever need anything we are in your debt."

"Well, now you come to mention it…." started Noggin who was in a daze dreaming about becoming a Night Warrior herself but was quickly stopped by Snitch stamping on her foot to shut her up.

"What happened in there?" asked Fitz looking towards the closed vault door. "What was that awful noise and what happened to your men?" as he looked at their battered armour and bleeding wounds.

"They deserve to know" replied Quillion Quartz.

"Everything you have just seen and heard you must never speak about outside this vault," said Bysidian sternly. All three nodded in agreement.

218

"As you know the whole time my team were inside the pearl fighting the nightmare within and believe me this was one of the worst nightmares we have ever had to battle. It got stronger and stronger as Solomon Fear tried to release it. The pearls protect the nightmares like treasure and will do all they can to stop us defeating what's inside and destroying it forever. The sound you heard was the pearl wailing as the battle was won and my Warriors escaped. Once they escape the pearl explodes in a pool of light and vanishes."

Fitz stood silent for a moment. "All the pearls in there lining the walls, the ones we bring home when we capture nightmares in the Dream Catcher Pearls every night, you have to do this with everyone?" Bysidian nodded slowly.

"SO" interrupted Noggin stepping forward amazed by this "I have to ask what the nightmare inside the pearl was?" With that Snitch stamped on her other foot hard and put his hands over his ears.

219

"LA, LA, LA, I don't want to know the answer to that question" he cried as Noggin hopped around with two sore feet.

They watched as the chuckling Night Warrior team along with Bysidian Black walked from the vault and disappeared from view, who knows when to be seen again.

Chapter 29

Oh No Not Again!

Ember dropped into the Dell with her three weary passengers, night had fallen. The tiny houses had lights shimmering in the windows with thin curls of smoke rising from the chimneys as the people of the dell settled in for the night. After a hug from a very sleepy Noggin and a pat from a half-asleep Snitch, she left them for her warm, dry bed to rest.

"Sleep well" called Noggin after her as she flew away.

Fitz watched as Noggin and Snitch disappeared out of view walking across the stream, dodging the flickering tiny dew dancers who were returning home from their nights work, and off to find their cosy beds to dream of the adventure none of them knew would happen when they woke that morning.

Fitz turned and was about to open his door when he spotted a small parcel wrapped in newspaper and tied with string on the doorstep, the label read:

I heard you may be missing one or two of

these.

The High Minister.

Undoing the neatly tied string Fitz looked at the newspaper wrapping.

TERROR AT THE TOWER

All is well at the Tower of London today after what was thought to be an attempted robbery last night. However, it is believed that one of the guards on duty carelessly fell asleep and woke to stumble into the security surrounding the Crown Jewels setting off The Towers alarms.

It is believed that whilst still half asleep he banged his head on one of the glass display cases smashing it.

Fortunately, the jewels inside were not damaged and nothing appears to have been stolen.

The Queen is said to be extremely relieved.

"Oh, if only they knew" yawned Fitz. "And with that, I think it's time for bed".

Fitz opened one blurry eye slowly under the warm soft covers where his face was buried deep in his pillow, he had been having a wonderful dream so what was that annoying noise......

"OH NO NOT AGAIN!!!!!"

Watch out for these other titles …

If you have a moment to spare, please leave a review on
Amazon.
Your help with spreading the world of the Dream Drifters
would be greatly appreciated.

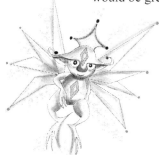

dianebanhamimagine@outlook.com
Facebook @DianeBanhamAuthor
Instagram @dianebanham

Printed in Great Britain
by Amazon

51161212R00135